HIGHLAND SONG

TANYA ANNE CROSBY

Second Edition

Created with Vellum

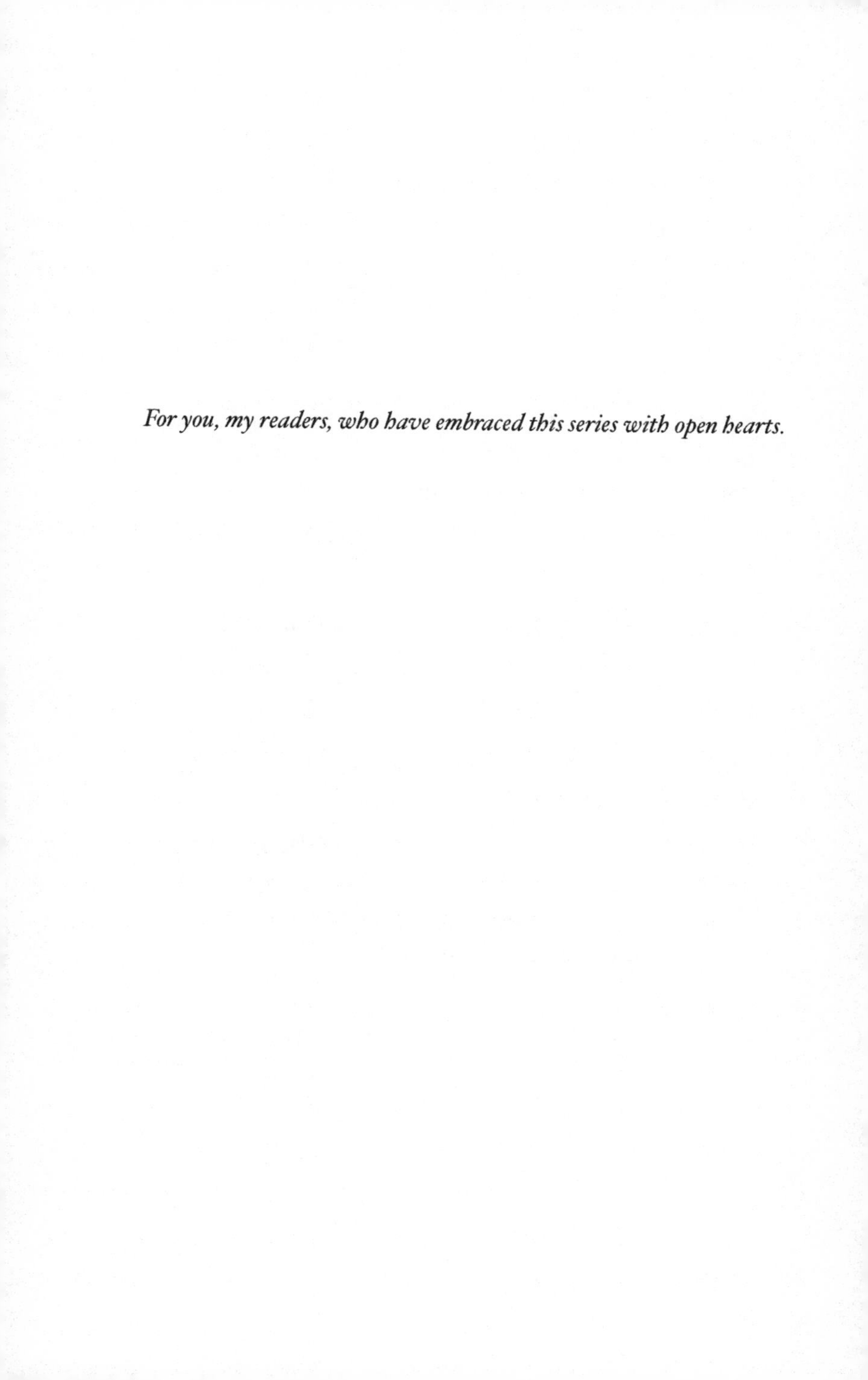

For you, my readers, who have embraced this series with open hearts.

PRAISE FOR TANYA ANNE CROSBY

"Crosby's characters keep readers engaged..."

— PUBLISHERS WEEKLY

"Tanya Anne Crosby sets out to show us a good time and accomplishes that with humor, a fast paced story and just the right amount of romance."

— THE OAKLAND PRESS

"Romance filled with charm, passion and intrigue..."

— AFFAIRE DE COEUR

"Ms. Crosby mixes just the right amount of humor... Fantastic, tantalizing!"

— RENDEZVOUS

"Tanya Anne Crosby pens a tale that touches your soul and lives forever in your heart."

— SHERRILYN KENYON #1 NYT BESTSELLING AUTHOR

SERIES BIBLIOGRAPHY

These books are ALSO AVAILABLE AS AUDIOBOOKS

START WITH THE MACKINNON'S BRIDE FREE

THE HIGHLAND BRIDES

The MacKinnon's Bride

Lyon's Gift

On Bended Knee

Lion Heart

Highland Song

MacKinnon's Hope

THE GUARDIANS OF THE STONE

Once Upon a Highland Legend

Highland Fire

Highland Steel

Highland Storm

Maiden from the Mist

ALSO CONNECTED...

Angel of Fire

Once Upon a Kiss

DAUGHTERS OF AVALON

The King's Favorite

A Winter's Rose

Fire Song

Rhiannon

MEDIEVAL SCOTLAND

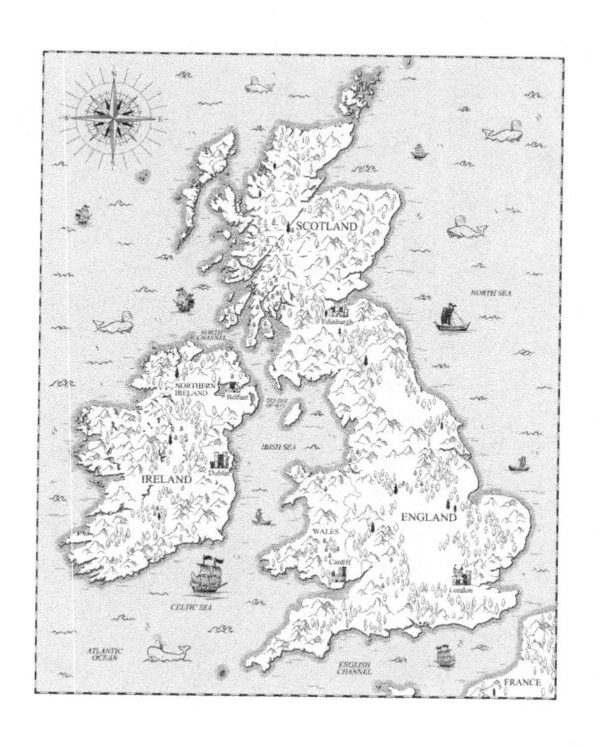

CHAPTER 1

THE HIGHLANDS OF SCOTIA, 1125

Gavin Mac Brodie was certain there was something amiss with Seana's *whiskie*.

Somehow, the woman had managed to snare the very last man in the Highlands Gavin would have thought might ever wed. During his brother's seven and twenty years, he had bedded more women than the entire Brodie clan had fingers to count on. But even more amazing was the simple fact that Colin was drunk with joy over the end of his promiscuity. His eyes followed his new wife wherever she went, mooning over her in a way that Gavin found quite embarrassing.

Good thing he wasn't a drinker, because he sure as hell didn't need a woman to lead him about by his nose. Everywhere he looked there was yet a new bride—the MacKinnon laird with his new English missus, Gavin's brother Leith and Alison MacLean, his sister Meghan and Piers de Montgomerie. And now Montgomerie's cousin Elizabet and Broc

Ceannfhionn—another fellow Gavin would never have imagined susceptible to the wiles of women.

Having reached his limit over so much mooning, he was compelled to seek solace in the forest where Seana had once made her home with her father. Her potstill was still there, a stone's throw away, because she had refused to move it, despite his brother's persistence. Seana claimed the spot held special magik necessary to a good brew. So she came every day to check the *whiskie*. But that didn't matter to Gavin; he could handle Seana well enough—even if he thought her bent toward the mystical was a bunch of malarkey.

He'd had enough of fair folk stories to last a lifetime. Like Seana, his Grandminny Fia had been keen to the old ways. She too had lived close to nature, loving the forest and dragging his sister Meggie out with her every opportunity. Together they had brewed concoctions of meadowsweet, bloodroot and heather and sometimes shoved them down his and his brothers' throats when they were ill. That was all well and good, but as far as Gavin was concerned, things like the will-o'-the-wisps were naught more than bugs. The still folk were little more than legends and the banshee were simply tales auld women told to make the wee ones behave.

All these women and their folklore... it was, indeed, enough to drive a man to drink, though dipping into Seana's witch's brew wouldn't get his house built any faster and he was bound and determined to get out of the lovebirds' ways, even if he broke his back with the labor.

Once the house was completed, he was certain no one would stop him from leaving, but he couldn't take the chance that they might try. He didn't want to continue living with his brothers, and certainly didn't care to hear the sounds of their lovemaking echoing through the halls all night long. Lying alone in his bed, there was nothing more disturbing.

CHAPTER 2

He'd fainted.

Like a pasty-faced milksop.

What would his brothers say?

With a groan of surprise, Gavin blinked at the pair of willowy legs in front of his face. Dazed, he followed the lithe line of her limbs up to the vee in her torso, and then groaned once more and quickly looked past the fiery curls to the face that stared down at him with unrepressed curiosity. Her arms were folded across her lovely breasts, concealing them for the moment. "I ha'e never seen a mon do that," she remarked.

"Och, me either," Gavin confessed. "You must've hexed me, woman!" Muttering an oath, he lifted himself to a seated position, afraid to look up again for fear of seeing her bits.

She tapped her foot. "Well, then, it'd serve ye right to call up the wrath of the dead." Her voice was full of ire. "Are ye accusing me of witchery?"

"Aye!" he said petulantly as he was certain that she was, indeed, a witch, despite that he didn't believe in magik. Nay, but her brand of witchery was purely feminine, and he found himself as hard as the stones he had used to erect his house.

Shifting, he hid his erection from her prying eyes, taking another circumspect look at her.

For all that she stood in the flesh—literally—she looked very much like the ghost of their ancestors. Had he somehow summoned her? But nay. His brain was addled still. He did not believe in the supernatural.

She stooped to inspect him, and he leapt up and away, taken aback by the unexpected intimacy. Christ, but if he'd needed proof that warm blood coursed through her veins, he got it then for he'd felt the heat of her body acutely.

"Och, lass, dinna ye have any shame?"

She looked nonplussed. Her brows collided. "Shame?"

He waved a hand at her, indicating her nude body. "You're no' wearing any bluidy clothes!" he said, pointing out what anybody with two good eyes could plainly see.

"So I'm not," she allowed and sounded entirely bemused by his observation. Her delicate brows arched. "Does it unsettle you?"

Without stopping to think about it, Gavin removed his tunic, desperate to see her clothed. "Aye! It does!" he confessed and tossed the garment at her feet. "Please, for the love of Christ, put that on!"

As a courtesy—not that he hadn't already seen nearly every exquisite inch of her—he looked away to give her privacy while she dressed, and in his peripheral, while he fixed his gaze upon his own feet, he saw that she shrugged and bent to pick up the green tunic. "Very well," she relented.

"Where are your clothes?"

"Why do ye care?" She lifted her arms and the tunic over her head.

Gavin's gaze returned helplessly to the swell of her bosom as she shimmied into the English styled tunic that likely still held his warmth. Her slim hips wiggled as she pulled it down of thighs or his tongue was deep in a jug of *whiskie*. Not much else had pleased him. Gavin and Meghan, being the youngest, had mostly been spared his heavy hand, while Leith had borne the brunt of their Da's temper.

As for poor Colin... their Da had dragged him out by the collar wherever he went carousing. As a result, his middle brother had learned the ways of women long before most of their peers had come out from beneath their minny's skirts. It should have made for a poor husband, but Colin was surprising them all with Seana.

For his part, Leith drove himself and everyone else to death's bloody doorstep in pursuit of perfection. Alison MacLean, with her crossed eyes, was the last woman any of them would have suspected he would lose his heart to. And yet he had.

In fact, both his brothers had wed women who, while lovely, would be deemed by their father's standards as less than perfect.

Gavin wasn't necessarily drawn to beauty and in fact he believed beauty reared demons of another sort—had Meggie not suffered enough over hers? Like their mother and grandmother before her, his sister had borne the biting tongue of women for leagues. "Mad Meghan Brodie" they had called her, and only Lyon Montgomerie—a Sassenach—had ever had the balls to match wits with his canny sister. Gavin had to chuckle over that, for it seemed to him that, despite the claims that her husband was a beast on the battlefield, in his sister's presence, Montgomerie was naught more than a hapless pussycat.

Come to think of it, he wondered where all the cats had gone to today. They had all simply disappeared. Unbidden, his thoughts returned to the painted lady...

She was certainly beautiful, though not in a conventional way, but she wasn't his, he reminded himself—nor was he looking to fill his bed. Nay, he had too many other things to concern himself with right now. He had not spent his entire life fighting his Da's influences only to succumb to them now. If, indeed, he ever did wed, he wanted a sweet Highland lass —not too beautiful, but pleasing to the eye—someone who was loyal and passionate and full of love. Someone who was soft-hearted and meek but strong in body with a song in her heart.

Anyway, he would likely never see the girl again. She'd fled without even telling him her name, and he doubted, despite her claim to rights, that she was from anywhere near these parts.

From the hall, the sound of voices and laughter drifted to his ears, but the female voices were new to this house. It filled him with a strange void. He sighed, giving his bower a long look. This house where he had lived his entire life had grown quite crowded. Everything was changing. He missed the fresh blooms Meggie had kept in his chamber... the way she had fluffed his pillow and kept the brazier burning in anticipation of his return. Now both his brothers had wives to warm their beds and breasts to lay their heads upon and his own room was dark and cold.

A sudden image of his painted lady came to mind... she was standing in the house he was building... the two of them preparing to sup together... her face aglow by the fire in the hearth and her wavy hair tied at her nape, like a fire bound by magik twine. Her lips turned gently at the corners and she laughed, the sound musical and free.

He blinked and the image disappeared.

Och, but he didn't want a wife, he told himself and turned from his bower and from the vision, heading toward the hall.

Wafting from the same direction as the voices, the peppery scent of haggis teased the air. Gavin followed the scent, ready for a wholesome meal after a long day's work.

Colin stopped shoving the haggis along the sides of his dish and Leith set down his tankard of ale.

"Really?" Leith asked.

Gavin glanced at Seana, hoping that she would know who the woman was. "Aye. She was tiny and lovely, with flaming hair and shining green eyes."

Seana laughed. "Mayhap she's one of the fair folk," she quipped and winked at him.

Gavin tried again. "No... but she was... er... well, painted..."

Seana frowned. "Painted?"

"Tattoos," Gavin clarified, waving a hand around his chest. "She had them everywhere."

Seana's gaze followed the circular movement of his fingers across his chest, her brow furrowing a little deeper. "Everywhere?"

Realizing suddenly where he was pointing, he indicated his arms instead. "Aye, well ye know... her arms, legs, face..." Her breasts, too, of course, and the memory made him flush. "She was blue," he finished uncomfortably, and cleared his throat.

Alison screwed her face and repeated dumbly. "She was blue?"

Gavin frowned. "Well, not her... her tattoos."

"Sounds to me like a bluidy Pecht," Leith suggested, "Though their kind have not been seen in an age."

"Fie on you two—Pechts and faeries!" Alison scolded. She turned to Gavin, giving him her full attention. "Tell me, where did you meet this... blue... painted lady?" she asked, making polite conversation.

Gavin winked at Seana. "Out near where Seana used to live with her Da."

Only Seana knew what he was doing out there and she

was sworn to secrecy—at least until he was ready to reveal his secret.

"Oh," Alison said, and attempted to split off a piece of her bread. Her nails found no purchase and she glowered, inspecting the object in her hand. "What were you doing all the way out there?" she asked, though distracted now. She knocked the piece of bread discreetly upon the table, peering circumspectly at Seana.

Gavin had the distinct impression that Seana was responsible for the bread as well—poor lass. She was accustomed to cooking over an open flame, for she and her Da had never had many conveniences.

He glanced from Seana to Alison and then from Alison to Seana. As far as his own house was concerned, he wasn't quite ready to tell anyone. Not yet. So he lied. "I was checking the potstill."

Alison sounded even more perplexed. She stopped inspecting her piece of bread rock. "I thought you didna approve of Seana's *whiskie*?"

Gavin cast Seana a beleaguered glance, hoping she did not take offense. "I dinna disapprove, I simply dinna want to drink it for myself. Anyway, I was oot there... near... so I decided to check on it... for Seana—that's all."

Seana peered down uncomfortably at her plate. She remained silent, avoiding everyone's gaze, and Gavin thought she might be uncomfortable abetting a lie.

Now it seemed it was Colin's turn to be confused. His haggis suddenly forgotten, he studied Gavin's face. "What were you doing out in No Mon's Land, brother?"

"Och! Colin! That is *not* no man's land!" Seana argued at once. "It is *my* land! I do so wish you'd stop calling it that! If you must know, I asked Gavin to check on the potstill for me," she lied.

"In any case," Gavin continued, feeling guilty for Seana's

sake. He peered at Leith, who was studying him now as well. "That's where I saw her."

"Who?" Alison asked absently as she tapped her biscuit once again upon the table.

The bluidy thing sounded like a hammer—Christ, but a mon could split his teeth on that.

Gavin set his own biscuit down upon his plate, abandoning it. "That's what I was hoping Seana might know..."

"Do you at least know her name?" Seana pressed. "Mayhap she is one of the MacKinnon's? That or Broc Ceannfhionn sometimes has cousins who wander by on their way up the bluff."

"Well, nay."

Colin's brows furrowed. "Nay, she was not a MacKinnon? Or nay ye dinna know her name?" he persisted.

Frustrated, Gavin cast his brother a glare. "Now, why would I be askin' aboot the lass if I knew from whence she hailed? Nay, I dinna know her name!" he said, losing patience.

"Why not?" Leith persisted.

Gavin was beginning to feel as though he were in the middle of an inquisition. "Because I didna ask is all!"

"Why not?"

"Och, because I was distracted!"

Colin slid Gavin a knowing grin. His brother knew him too well. Still he asked, "By what?"

Gavin's cheeks heated and he said defensively, "By the potstill, o' course!"

"Of course," Colin allowed, looking smug.

Seana continued to play along. "Well, so... how was it?"

Gavin blinked, feeling dizzier now than he had in the girl's presence. "How the hell was what?"

Now even Seana narrowed her eyes at him. "The *whiskie*, Gavin! The *whiskie*!"

Suddenly, Alison dropped her biscuit and slapped a hand to her forehead. "I'm so verra confused!"

Leith turned to put an arm around her shoulders and offered her a kiss upon the cheek. "That makes two of us, my dear."

Colin, the cur, merely lifted a brow and his wicked grin spread wider. "Seems to me as though you've been in the sun too long, little brother?"

"Indeed you have," Seana rushed to add. "Your face is the color of beets!"

Colin tapped her on the nose lovingly, and said, "That, my lovely wife, is called a virgin's blush." And he turned to give Gavin a knowing wink.

For the quip and for the wink, Gavin gave Colin a sour look, and having had quite enough of their ribbing, he raked his chair back from the table, certain that this conversation could go nowhere productive. "I dinna believe I am hungry after all," he said and gave Brownie a whistle before quitting the hall.

The dog bounded after him.

"Bastard," Leith said, but without meaning.

"What do you suppose that was all about?" Alison asked once Gavin had departed.

Colin stared at the door from whence Gavin had gone. "Were it not for those bluidy vows of his, I would think our brother was in lust."

Alison screwed her face. "Nay! Not Gavin!" she assured.

"Och," Colin argued. "I vow that boy's blood is as red as mine."

"Aye, well, he might be your little brother," Alison rebuked with a lifted brow, "but Gavin hasna been a boy for quite some time in case ye havena noticed."

Seana gave them all a knowing smile and shrugged. "Could be he got into the *whiskie*," she said softly.

CHAPTER 3

Outside, the moon was high and full, illuminating the courtyard well enough for Gavin to see behind the little chapel, where he spied lovers kissing beneath the moonlight, their limbs obscured by the rising mist. From this distance, he could only see their silhouettes, and couldn't make out who they were. It didn't matter; it seemed everyone had found someone but him.

He sat with his back to a stack of logs and Brownie laid dutifully at his feet. Petting the dog's back absently, he tried not to think of anything at all.

Sometimes, it did a mon good to clear his brain and feed his soul—never mind his belly, grumble though it may.

He had no idea how long he sat there, but after awhile Seana appeared at his side. "You must be starved," she said quietly, surprising him. Sometimes, it seemed she was made of mist, so silently did she appear. It must be a consequence of living in the forest, without the benefit of protection, and having to fend so long for herself, Gavin decided.

She wrapped Colin's tartan about her shoulders and sat gingerly upon the pile of logs beside him.

Gavin shrugged. Indeed, he was hungry, but he planned to sneak back into the kitchen after everyone was asleep, so as not to hurt anyone's feelings—most especially not Seana's for he had grown to care for the lass.

"Ye look lovely in Brodie colors," he told her and meant it. "It suits you."

Seana lifted her shoulders, hugging the blanket possessively and smiling warmly. "Thank you, dear Gavin." She tilted him a look, confessing, "The haggis was bad, I know. But I'm afraid me and Da made do with simpler fare."

He gave her a sympathetic look. "Do ye miss him still?"

She nodded. "Nary a day goes by that I don't, but I know he's out there somewhere... watching o'er me."

"It's good to have faith," he said, though he couldn't seem to find any for himself these days. "Dinna fret, lass. For a time, even Meggie burned everything after Grandminny Fia passed."

Her tone was hopeful. "Truly?"

"Aye, my brothers and I were doubled over for weeks with hunger pangs. We worked through supper and snuck into the kitchen when the moon was high. And Colin, the bastard, hoarded all the bluidy bread—the one thing Meggie knew how to do right."

Seana giggled at the image he presented—all three brothers sneaking about in the middle of the night for victuals. "The Colin I know has always been a wee bit of a brat," she agreed.

Gavin lifted both his brows. "A wee bit?"

Seana giggled again.

"Where are they now?"

"Colin and Leith?" She gave him a canny look. "Alison has them both cleaning out the hearth.

Gavin laughed. "Smart lass," he said, but left it at that.

Above them, the stars winked like brilliant jewels in a

clear ebony sky, despite the thick mist that swirled low to the ground. It was this sort of evening when the woods seemed almost surreal, full of blinking eyes and snapping twigs, unseen footsteps and whispers. The sort of night when a body could actually believe in faeries and wraiths. His Grandminny Fia had certainly believed in their existence, and she had walked about talking to them even in the broad light of day. Alas, it had earned her the first of the Mad Brodie titles. He glanced up at Seana, wondering if Seana and Alison would break that curse for Brodie women at long last.

Seana wrapped her cloak about her more firmly against the night air and demanded suddenly, "Tell me about this woman you met today, Gavin."

Gavin peered up at her. She was quite lovely, his brother's wife. It was no wonder Colin was enamored with her. And she had a heart of gold besides. Though she wasn't anything at all like his painted lady.

He shrugged. "Not much to tell. I simply wondered if ye had e'er seen her," he explained, peering up to gauge her expression.

"Mayhap she was looking for a husband?" She winked at him. "After all, there isna a woman for leagues who doesna fancy herself a Brodie bride."

"Nay. They do not pine for me," Gavin assured her. "Leith is head of his clan. 'Tis quite natural a woman would fancy him, and Colin... well, 'tis no mystery what ladies might see in my pretty brother... but nay, no' me."

Seana chuckled. "Colin would not like it to hear himself called pretty, I think. But I can assure you there is no' a woman in these Highlands who would not pluck oot her eyes to be your bride."

He gave her a half-hearted grin. "If she plucked oot her eyes, then she wouldna have to see me—is that what ye're thinking?"

Both of them laughed, and Brownie began to lick his paw, chewing at his nails.

"I have nothing much to offer," Gavin said, this time without levity.

"Hmmm," Seana replied and looked down upon him with furrowed brows. After a long moment of contemplation, she added. "My Da was of the mind that those woods oot there are full of magik. He was certain my minny was a faerie... that he would join her once he passed this world to the next. In fact, the last few years of his life, he swore she was a cat—My Love, he'd called her."

"A cat?"

Seana rolled her eyes. "And I half believed it, because it seemed that bluidy cat was always aboot."

"What do you believe now?" Gavin asked.

Seana shrugged. "Well... I believe there are things we canna explain," she confessed.

"Like what?"

She grinned down at him. "Like love, Gavin Mac Brodie. If love is not some form of magik, then I dunno what is."

She stood then and shivered, wrapping her tartan more securely about her shoulders. "You should come in soon," she suggested. And then added. "I'll make sure Alison isna aboot the kitchen so ye can grab yersel' a snack—and dinna worry for my feelings one bit."

She left him with a smile and another wink.

Thereafter, Gavin sat alone, contemplating her words, and the meaning of life. He stared at the little church they had built some years ago to their grandminny's displeasure.

In fact, the structure had once been an ancient cairn—a particularly large one that had long been sacked. Gavin had shored up the walls with good sturdy beams and had constructed a timber roof.

"You'll anger the gods!" Fia had railed. *"What has this world*

come to!" And she would walk away, mumbling to herself about the arrogance of youth.

Unlike the chapel Meggie had begun for him on Montgomerie land, this one was simply a private place to bend the knee and pray—something he rarely did these days, as he seemed to have lost his way.

That's what the girl had said today, though how would she know? Lucky guess is all.

He sighed, knowing full well that in the past he had annoyed his siblings with his affinity for scripture. And yet they had let him speak his heart. Looking back on it now, he was not so certain he understood the desperation behind his studies, though he thought it had something to do with the turmoil in his soul—that emptiness he could not seem to fill no matter how many good deeds he carried out. Or mayhap it was just a safe diversion.

Love?

Magik!

Humph.

He stood, scooping up a stone into his hand as he watched the lovers behind the church hie away into the privacy of the woods and felt an unexpected stab of envy.

Tossing the stone halfheartedly in the direction of the new storehouse they were building, he went inside, determined to finish his house within the week. Of late, it was the one thing that gave him a sense of satisfaction. After weeks of working on it, he was so close. Only the roof must be raised, and then he would begin the well. Once that was done, and he was prepared to till the land, then he would appeal to his brother Leith to trade him a few of the sheep and goats in return for part of his spring harvest.

Aye, and that gave him a warmth in his breast that not even Seana's *whiskie* could touch.

As for love... some things were not meant for everyone, he supposed.

As for his painted lady, she was long gone by now, and he'd best cast the image of her out of his mind once and for all. It would serve no purpose to lose his heart over a woman, who, for all practical purposes, did not exist—no matter how lovely those painted breasts were.

❧

GAVIN SPENT THE NEXT TWO DAYS HELPING HIS BROTHERS with the construction of the new storehouse. Neither the MacLeans nor the Brodies were as prosperous as Iain MacKinnon, but their clearings were hardly insubstantial, and every last man and woman must do their part.

Once finished, his new house would be a modest home made of good, sturdy mortared stone—hardly any bigger than a common hovel, but that suited Gavin just fine.

In these parts, only the MacKinnon laird had any sort of stronghold. Seated at the top of the bluff, *Chreagach Mhor* held the envy of every neighboring clan, for it rivaled even the holdings of the sons of Malcom Ceann Mór.

Luckily for David—the youngest of Malcom's sons—Iain MacKinnon had no designs on the throne of Scotia, for with David's nose so far up the English King's arse it wouldn't take very much to incite the people against him. And with a bloodline that hailed straight back to Kenneth MacAlpin, Iain would surely gain the ear of every Highlander were he to give a care. Thus it was no surprise to anyone that David suddenly seemed to be Iain's staunchest ally. Anything the MacKinnon decreed, David echoed from the blufftops though it was certainly not that way for all of the claimants to the throne.

Some had met other fates.

Trying to bar the image of his lady's lovely painted body from his thoughts, Gavin laid more stone during the next two days than he had in all the weeks he'd been working on his new house.

All three brothers worked side by side to build the new storehouse because, for once, the old one had been filled long before the coming winter. In part because the neighboring clans had begun to work together to trade supplies. The MacKinnons had an expert candle maker, whose candles burned true and bright, the MacLeans could grow tatties in just about any nook or cranny, the Brodies were all excellent farmers and sheep herders, and Piers de Montgomerie had Sassenach family to trade with in England. Gavin's sister Meghan was an expert weaver, and her cloth was tight and soft. Now, the Brodies had Seana, as well, and some of the best *whiskie* in all the Highlands.

All in all this was shaping up to be the most plentiful winter they'd had since long before their father had led their clan. Their grandsire, for all his wenching, had been an excellent laird.

Gavin was only slightly concerned that Seana's claim might come under scrutiny, for it would give the Brodies a stretch of land that had not been theirs previously. And yet, now that there was peace between the clans, and his sister's husband owned the property adjacent to the south, and the Brodies owned the property adjacent to the west, he was certain that once he stood before the clan councils no one would deny him, particularly if he gained the MacKinnon's favor—which he planned to seek at once. But he didn't foresee that the MacKinnon would have much dispute with the request for Seana's father had occupied the lands below the cliffs of *Chreagach Mhor* for all his life, and Seana was now wed to his eldest brother, laird of the Brodie clan.

At any rate, the clans all regarded that particular stretch

of property as No Mon's Land, as it was hardly the most fertile ground to be had. As it was, the key to his success as a farmer would be in the dowsing of a new well—something he wasn't particularly looking forward to doing. He hadn't known a good diviner since his Grandminny Fia, and he didn't relish the thought of boring holes through that craggy clay to find a plentiful water supply.

Despite working shoulder to shoulder with his brothers, somehow, Gavin managed to get through the day without drawing questions about his visits to No Man's Land or his mystery woman. Unfortunately, that was partly because one entire section of the new storehouse wall collapsed. Luckily for Gavin, it was Colin's stretch of wall. Even now, his brother couldn't seem to keep his eyes off his lovely wife.

Silly besotted fool.

At first light the following morning, while Colin repaired his damages, Gavin set out to speak to the MacKinnon. He found the entire MacKinnon household all up in arms over some escaped prisoner of King David's—a woman, Gavin discovered, and he couldn't help but think about his painted lady.

This prisoner, it seemed, was the sister of a rebel chieftain from deep in the Mounth—a rough range of hills in the northeast. She was to become a ward of the English King—much as they had attempted to do with Iain's firstborn son. Apparently, Iain had refused to join the search, because his wife was currently in labor, but Gavin knew there was more to that story.

For Gavin's part, it seemed his timing couldn't have been poorer. After what had happened to Iain's first wife, he wondered over the wisdom in waiting for counsel with him. If the labor didn't go well, Iain wouldn't be fit to speak. On the other hand, if the outcome was good, and the MacKinnon was gifted with a healthy bairn, and his new wife didn't commit self murder as his first wife had done, well then, he was sure to be pleased and in a generous mood.

With bated breath, he waited with Broc Ceannfhionn to hear the news, all the while Broc and his wife Elizabet argued over what to name their own child.

Gavin had to scratch his head over that one, because the sweet little babe was nearly six months auld.

"What do you call her now?" he asked Broc.

Broc frowned. "Babe."

His wife placed a platter of sweets upon the table and prompted Gavin to take one. He didn't hesitate, hungry as he was these days without a proper cook about the manor. "I want to name her Suisan," his wife said in her gentle English accent. "'Tis a lovely name, don't you think so?" she inquired of Gavin.

Not wanting to take sides, Gavin bit into his tart and glanced at Broc, who was frowning all the more intensely now. The nose Broc's dog Merry had broken sniffed with disapproval.

"Gavin is *my* friend," Broc pointed out to his wife. "Ye canna campaign for his agreement. That's not the way 'tis done!"

The expression upon Elizabet's face was quite guileless, but her smile was calculating, although Broc, for the moment, seemed unaffected by both. "It's a perfectly lovely name," she contended, ignoring his assertion.

To Broc's credit, he shook his head, holding his ground—unlike his brothers who would have both capitulated at once. Mayhap there was hope for these men in love after all? Perhaps all that was needed was time to temper both his brothers' moods?

Gavin shoved another sweet into his mouth, and took the opportunity to chew vigorously, thereby saving himself from having to respond to either of them.

Still smiling, Elizabet advanced upon her husband and sat upon his lap. Gavin's cheeks heated as they began to whisper and peck each others' faces, and he stood up to peer out the window at the MacKinnon's immense stone keep, wondering how long before they received word from the tower above.

That tower was the very same from which his first wife had flung herself from in fury.

"Och, verra well," he heard Broc say.

Gavin shook his head over the futility of men in love. By the saints, all that was truly needed to conquer these Highlands was a parcel of Sassenach women. The MacKinnon had two in his midst already—his own wife and now Elizabet. It seemed they were as good as Sassenachs already. But it was none of his concern; all he cared about right now was securing the lands below the bluff to farm.

Suddenly, there was a shout from the tower window—a joyous cry, and Gavin rushed outside to hear what was being hailed.

Apparently, everyone else had been waiting to hear as well for the houses all emptied into the courtyard below.

"A girl!" the midwife shouted from the high window. "A wee baby girl!" And then she disappeared again.

So Gavin waited, happily, and much to his good fortune, the MacKinnon had nary a single reservation about his request. He sent Gavin away with his blessings and an imprint of his massive hand upon the small of Gavin's back.

Gavin had to wonder how any man would dare defy the MacKinnon for any reason. Like his father before him, he was a mighty force to be reckoned with.

As soon as the search party left the woods, Catrìona returned to the little house, hoping to hide within, thinking that even if the owner returned, he had been kind enough to offer her something to wear. Mayhap he would offer her a safe haven as well?

In return, she had been willing to help him complete his roof—something every woman in her clan knew how to do as no one was treated any differently simply because one had an appendage dangling between one's legs. She had been raised to earn her keep, and this was no different.

She hoped that because the Scot lived alone—or at least she supposed he did—he might not realize they were searching for her. Those devils had bound her and stripped her but she had managed to escape. Och but she'd rather die than become a pawn to subdue the last of her people! She had so little faith in these leaders of Scotia.

But she couldn't return home either—not yet.

It had worked out better than she anticipated. The owner of the house had yet to return, but when he did there would be no need to ask him if he wanted her help—no need to weather his dubious expressions, for she was nearly finished now, and he would surely not refuse her a place to sleep once he saw all the work she had done for him.

The thatch was good and tight—as she had been taught to weave it—so that it would not leak even with the halest of storms.

He was quite sweet—the Scot. And handsome besides—just the sort of man she might have wanted to wed some day. His blond hair was thick and clean. His jaw was well defined, with just the tiniest hint of a cleft. His green eyes were as deep and dark as moss—but most of all they were kind.

However, he had obviously forgotten how to dress like a man. The gown he had given her was lovely, but she wasn't accustomed to seeing men in embroidered dresses.

Then again, neither was she accustomed to running about naked as the day she was born either, but she wasn't ashamed of the body she had been given—fie on them! As though that should stop her from trying to escape their greasy clutches.

As for her Scot... he had barely been able to take his eyes off her breasts, and the memory made her smile. Truly, she would never have even painted herself, save that it was an act of defiance. It was her way of showing them that she would never bend to the will of these arrogant curs—and neither would her kinsmen. They had survived wave after wave of pillages from the north, and the endless politicking of the Highland tribes after the son's of Aed and Constantine had returned from Ireland two centuries past. Nay, but her people were survivors, and they would never abandon the old ways. She would keep her faith until the last frail breath left her lungs for she was a child of Alba, a sister to the wind and a daughter of the forest.

Humming while she worked, she inspected the dagger the Scot had left. It was a fine dagger, much like the one her brother had given her when she was ten. The bastards had taken that from her too. She wanted it back.

She sighed and tossed the dagger down. It landed precisely where she intended it to land, in the heart of the log where the Scot had been sitting when she found him, drinking from his flagon.

Diabhul, he was a beautiful man!

A man who wore dresses, but beautiful nevertheless.

She grinned at that, and returned to work, smoothing down the thatch that she had stolen from a nearby farm.

CHAPTER 4

It was growing dark by the time Gavin made his way off the blufftop, so he made his way home instead of dallying through the woods at night.

His grandminny had often told stories about a man who had been consigned to walk the earth for all eternity as a punishment for his crimes. That man had been allowed one grace, she'd said—a burning shard of pit coal to warm him and light his way. He used it instead to lead travelers along treacherous paths. That man she also claimed was responsible for the will-o'-the-wisp. On the other hand, his Da had sworn bog gas was responsible for the mysterious lights, not spirits or fair folk.

Whatever the truth of that matter, any man in his right mind knew to stay out of the forests at night in these parts—especially alone in these days of unrest.

The house could wait another day.

That night, he slept like a bairn, pleased that all had gone so well, and in the morning, once he verified that his brothers were not yet ready to renew efforts on the storehouse, he made a quick stop at the potstill to check on Seana's *whiskie.*

In truth, he had no clue what he was supposed to do if anything went awry—except to hie back and tell Seana. Her potstill was a complete mystery to him. Built by her late father, the only person who knew how to work the blamed thing was Seana herself. Luckily, everything seemed to be brewing as usual. The potstill was making all the familiar noises, chugging and spitting like an old man with phlegm in his throat, and fuming like his grandminny's pipe. Gavin winced over the smell and waved a hand before his nose.

Not surprisingly, this morning, there seemed to be a plethora of cats lolling about the still—black cats, white cats and more tabbies than he could shake a stick at. God's teeth, but he had never seen so many bluidy felines. If he didn't know better, he'd think they were all having a party with Seana's *whiskie*. With every day that passed, more and more congregated around the still. That didn't bode well for Brownie. His poor dog would surely lose his head around here. Resigned to the fact that his dog was like to be chasing cats for the rest of his given days, he continued on to the edge of the woods, singing a tune his grandminny had taught him when he was a boy.

O western wind when wilt thou blow
That the small rain down can rain?
Christ that my love were in my arms
And I in my bed again!

He didn't know any other verses, but he didn't much care. Soon his house would be completed and he couldn't wait to share the news. Three grown men under a single roof, along with wives, was simply too much to bear.

Still singing, he broke through the tree line, into the clearing, and for a moment, the sight before him didn't quite register. And then it did, and he stumbled in his step, blinking.

The house was already finished.

The roof had been raised.

His painted lady sat upon the rooftop, smoothing down the last of the thatch. "Good morn to you!" she bade him, waving the instant she spied him.

Gavin couldn't find his voice to speak.

For a moment, he wondered if the fumes from Seana's potstill could have had the same affect as her *whiskie* because he was nearly certain he was hallucinating.

He moved forward cautiously, mouth agape.

It was a damned good roof too—as good as any he had ever constructed—nay, better! But it wasn't even remotely possible. Even if she weren't a woman, a roof that size should have taken nearly a week to raise.

Nay, it wasn't possible.

"What is this?" he asked, peering up at her, waving a hand at the roof.

Undaunted, she glanced down at him, grinning, her cheeks revealing the tiniest dimples. "Well, I believe they call it a roof," she said smartly. "Do you like it?"

Did he like it?

Of course he liked it, but it was physically impossible for her to have completed it in the time since he'd been gone—particularly considering that she would have had to gather and bind the thatch. He stood staring at her, looking like a daft mon, he knew.

"Aye, but where the bluidy hell did it come from?"

She winked at him. "Faerie magik," she quipped and laughed, the sound as musical as a song. Then, more soberly she added, "'Tis my way of thanking you for this lovely dress."

"It's a tunic," he explained irascibly. "No' a bluidy dress! Do ye truly expect me to believe you simply blinked your pretty eyes and here it is?"

She shrugged and then scooted to the edge of the roof,

dangling her legs over the side and there she sat, beaming down at him, looking entirely too lovely, and swinging those bare legs—legs that were perfectly fit and lean.

Gavin averted his eyes, not daring to look up beyond her knees. Still, despite his resolve to be a gentleman, his cock stirred beneath his breacan. "Christ!" he said. "Come down from there! Come down right now!"

The paint upon her legs was gone today, as though she'd laved somewhere. Gavin tried not to think of her standing bare as the day she was born, washing in the loch, her long, graceful fingers caressing those perky breasts. His body tensed, and his blood began to sing in his veins.

"Nay," she refused. "Not 'til you say *go raibh maith agat*," she admonished, though still she smiled, and Gavin shook his head—not to refuse her request for a thank you but because he still could not believe his eyes.

"Di' ye do this all by yourself?" he asked, nonplussed, unable to move beyond the sudden appearance of a roof.

Her pale brows drew together. "Och, well, who else di' ye think would help?" She waved a hand. "All these bluidy cats?"

"Nay, but this is not possible!" he persisted, peering up to see that she was climbing down now, giving him a fine view of the moon of her arse as she made her way off the rooftop.

"By the good saints, lass, didn't your minny ever warn ye to keep your bits to yourself? It's bad manners!"

She stopped halfway down, legs dangling, holding herself up by those arms—firm arms that, like her legs, seemed accustomed to work. He could easily reach up and smooth his hand over her little rear to see if it felt as firm and smooth as it appeared. "My bits?"

Gavin waved her down, desperate to remove himself from temptation. "Never mind. Get down!" he demanded. "Get down!"

She dropped to the ground in front him, facing him

tongue far sharper than most blades and a wit twice as keen. "What now?" he asked.

Piers blew out a sigh, wondering the same.

In truth, he had never expected to find himself a laird and he was learning as he went how to deal with these canny Scots. He had come to truly admire them for they fought their battles by some strange code of honor that appealed to him. They stole your goat; you stole their sheep; and so on and so on—all of it done openly, as though thieving your good neighbor were the most natural and honorable thing to do. However, never accuse one without proof, he'd learned, for they defended kith and kin unto their dying breath. But the Brodie brothers had already come to accept him and he didn't believe they would resort to thieving anymore—particularly since this particular booty was intended to benefit the youngest of the brood.

Nay, something else was amiss here.

Scratching his head, he turned and walked out of the barn, into the bright sunshine, only to find riders approaching in the distance. He squinted to see the banner, and spied the bright gold with the royal blood red lion rampant at its center. King David. Despite his poor reputation in these parts, he rode with only a handful of men. Baldwin offered him a look that was full of trepidation for despite Piers' friendship with David, they both knew that David's presence here meant trouble.

Together they waited in the open field until the riders reined in before them.

At once Piers noted the scowls upon his mens' faces. "Your Grace... what brings you to these parts again so soon?" he asked.

Unsettled, like its rider, David's horse protested his weight and the anxious king dismounted. He came forward to kiss Piers quickly and stood before them, hands upon his hips. His men remained mounted, sour faced and sweating. "We brought a prisoner from the Mounth," he said without preamble. "A woman."

Piers frowned, as there were no women amongst them at the moment.

"We lost her," David said irritably, evidently guessing at Piers' thoughts. "The canny wench unbound herself when no one was looking and smacked Dùghall right upside the head." He inclined his head toward one of the men who sat, tense in his saddle, with a lump on his forehead the size of a man's bollocks.

"Christ," Piers said, though more as a response to the size of the lump on the man's noggin. "Who was she?" She had to be a hefty woman to leave a mark like that.

"The sister of a northern rebel chieftain. She was to become a ward of the English court until she was old enough to wed. Alas, she escaped before we could reach *Chreagach Mhor*!"

Piers was genuinely taken aback. "MacKinnon agreed to such a thing?" The MacKinnon laird he knew would no more be a part of such a scheme than he would have allowed his own son to remain a political pawn. He had, in fact, gone to great lengths to secure the return of his own son—including stealing the daughter of his foe to barter for his son's return. That he had made amends with David afterward was simply a testament to the MacKinnon's temperament—and the simple fact that he'd fallen deeply in love with his English bride. But Iain's good nature only went so far, and Piers was shocked that David would take such a risk again, when, King or not, his rule was not favored in these parts.

David's look darkened. Friends they might be, but he didn't like his edicts questioned. "We have yet to tell him exactly who she is," he confessed. And suddenly realizing Piers would wonder why he'd risked Iain's wrath when Piers was his strongest ally in these regions, he added. "*Chreagach Mhor* was the only stronghold we trusted to hold the wench until an escort arrived from London."

Piers knew better than to laugh. "You need a fortress to contain a girl?" He glanced again at the lump on Dùghall's forehead and came to his own conclusions, wisely holding his tongue.

David's furry brows collided. "I take it you have not seen her?"

Piers shook his head. "Nary a hair on her head."

"Damn! Well, we have searched everywhere! Though I cannot believe she would have ventured this way. I would have thought she'd attempt to fly away home."

Clearly, since they were alone, MacKinnon did not feel obligated to aid David's search. Piers considered the wisdom in offering his own aid, but felt obliged to offer his liege a place to stay at least.

"Alas, we cannot," David refused. "Should we find the lass we'll be needing the MacKinnon's gaol." He turned to calm his mount, stroking its withers. "I'll be picking hairs from betwixt my teeth with all the arse licking I must do—damned troublesome wench!"

Piers thought about Meghan's brothers, and how they had fought so desperately to bring their sister home. He wondered of the missing woman's family. Despite that it had worked out for him, he could no longer condone such heavy handed tactics as stealing a girl from her folk as these were flesh and blood people, not pawns on a chess board. "I'll keep an eye out for her," he promised as David remounted his steed. Though he sincerely hoped he would not see her.

David shook his head once he was mounted, and said again, "Damned troublesome wench!" And then giving his men a signal to depart, they hied away, leaving both Piers and Baldwin staring after them.

"I hate to say it," Baldwin ventured, knowing he could speak freely with Piers. "He might have bitten off more than he could chew when he claimed Scotia's throne. Peace between the clans will not come easily."

Piers watched his friend and liege disappear into the horizon and sighed heavily. "I don't know," he said, torn. "The land I hold was once the most precarious clearing of all, and yet we now have peace amongst the most querulous of the lot." He didn't have to condone it to admit the fact. "His strategy is quite brilliant, in fact. If he can marry them all off, he won't ever have to lift a sword against a one."

"True," Baldwin agreed.

"Although," Piers added soberly, "I pray he knows to tread softly as he goes as these are not the men to anger."

❧

Cat.

The name lifted Gavin's brows.

But it was just a coincidence, he reasoned. Simply because she had appeared from nowhere, looking for all the world like a graceful feline herself, didn't mean she was any sort of fair folk, changed from a cat.

And simply because she had raised his roof faster than any man he knew might have done it didn't mean she had done so with any sort of magik—nor had she spun the thatch that had appeared just as mysteriously as she had.

She wasn't a faerie.

Gavin didn't believe in such things. He had a hard enough time lately keeping his own faith.

At any rate, fair folk didn't eat the way she did—enough for a man twice her size.

At least he didn't think they would.

Seated together upon the same log, he shared his lunch

with Cat... or rather, he nibbled upon a single piece of cheese while he watched her gobble her food. He had spread his sack upon the ground and laid the contents out upon it for both of them to sup upon. However, considering that he had already eaten this morn and it was not yet nones, he wasn't very hungry yet. Cat, on the other hand, appeared as though she hadn't eaten for days. She sat, stuffing her gob faster than she could pluck the foodstuffs from the linen sack. Not since he had been a child with two brothers and a greedy sire at the table had he witnessed such a rush for every morsel.

"If I ate like that," Gavin told her, "I would be as big as this house." Not that it was a complaint. He was simply shocked, and having lived with two brothers and a very outspoken sister, he wasn't accustomed to holding his tongue.

She stopped in the midst of putting a bite of oatcake into her mouth and looked at him, her expression slightly horrified, as though only now realizing how quickly she had dispatched his lunch.

"Don't stop," he reassured her. "If you're hungry there's plenty more where this came from. I simply canna fathom how you stay so small."

Cat smiled, but not before shoving another bite into her lovely mouth. She swallowed, and then said, "My brother says 'tis because I am cursed with a joint eater."

"A joint eater?"

She leaned to whisper into his ear as though it were a secret. "One o' the invisible folk," she said. "They steal your food so ye canna benefit." She nodded, glanced at her side—where absolutely no one was seated—then placed a finger to her lips, as though to shush him.

Gavin stared at her, nonplussed. The entire situation was growing stranger by the instant.

She wasn't a cat. Nor was she a faerie. And she most

certainly wasn't sharing her food with some invisible goblin oatcake thief! He didn't believe it! Not for a moment.

"This is quite good!" she declared, plucking another bite of cheese and shoving it whole into her mouth.

Gavin couldn't resist a chuckle. Never in his life had he seen a woman eat with such unrestrained passion. Just to be sure she got enough, he pushed his portion closer to the middle. She stopped chewing, watching as he adjusted the foodstuff upon the sack, and then turned and gifted him with another of her brilliant smiles.

Gavin felt a flutter in his belly that soared clear into his chest. Damn, but if he could witness such a thing on a daily basis, he would gladly give up every meal.

"Thank you," she said softly. "Where I come from, if ye dinna fend for yourself, ye dinna eat at all."

"Me too," he confessed, and eyed her circumspectly. "So where did ye say that was?"

Since the moment she had first appeared, curiosity had been his constant companion.

She lifted her knees and put one arm about them as she spoke, hugging them like a child might. "Here and there," she said glibly, though her gaze shifted to peek at him from her peripheral.

She was hiding something.

He sensed it, and knew it had nothing to do with magik.

"Aye, well, I believe I've been there," he joked, realizing she was not going to tell him the truth anyway.

She laughed, and her toes—lovely little things—curled into the soil. Here, closer to the forest, the land was easier to till. But he wouldn't want to bring his garden too close, lest he lose full sun. Nor did he wish to tangle with all the many tree roots.

"What about you?" she asked. "Ha'e ye lived here all of your life?"

"Close," he replied, and he told her about his home, about his sister's marriage to a Sassenach—and the feud that had started everything. When Piers de Montgomerie had first claimed his clearing from David of Scotia, none of the surrounding clans had been accepting of the fact. In truth, Gavin had no idea who stole the first goat, but they had begun a feud to rival that of the MacKinnon's and MacLean's. In the end, Montgomerie had stolen their sister and then had promptly wed her—somehow earning Meggie's love in the process—not an easy task. As far as Gavin was concerned, that was all that mattered. If his sister was happy, so was he.

He told her about both his brothers and their weddings—how Leith's wife had first coveted Colin and how Seana had coveted Broc and all the while Colin wanted no woman at all. In the end, Colin was smitten with Seana and Leith lost his heart to Alison while Broc, who secretly had coveted his laird's wife, had wed a Sassenach cousin of Piers de Montgomerie.

The way she was looking at him suddenly made Gavin feel uncomfortable—as though she somehow sensed why he had been driven away from his home. She said not a word, but it was that shrewd look in her eyes—along with a touch of pity that was unfamiliar to him, except when he looked at himself through his own eyes.

He explained to her about his arrangement with Seana—so that she might better understand why he was here... away from his family. It wasn't simply because he couldn't bear to witness so much of something he would never have. Gavin was happy for his brothers and sister—truly pleased for them.

But he was two score and four years now, without ever having kissed a woman. He'd bedded only one, but regretted it immediately after, for once he'd quenched his body's hunger, she had fled, looking ashamed, and Gavin had let her go, not knowing exactly what to do because he hadn't loved her. He'd been just a lad with a crowing cock. And now every time they chanced to spy each other—especially in the presence of her husband—she averted her gaze.

Thereafter, Gavin had fought so hard to deny that part of himself his brother Colin and father seemed unable to resist. Though his brother's heart was true enough, Colin had somehow never noticed the tears that had spilled in his wake. But Gavin had, and his soul had cried along with every broken heart—because he remembered that terrible melancholy in the girl's eyes. And later, he had been so involved with his studies and scripture that women saw him coming and fled the other way. Even his sister Meggie grimaced over the prospect of a simple conversation with him, despite the little church she had built for him.

He hadn't realized how long he'd remained quiet, contemplating, until Cat broke the silence. "So Seana lived out here all alone?"

Gavin nodded. "With her Da... until she wed my brother Colin, aye." He waved in the direction of the forest. "Her potstill sits out yonder."

Cat tore a bite out of her oatcake, nodding. "I have seen it. Her *uisge beatha* has the scent of a verra good brew," she told him, using the old tongue for its name. "But I didna try it," she reassured. "'Tis verra bad luck to drink a new brew before the libation has been offered and I would never dare curse a mon's brew—or a woman's," she corrected herself, and giggled. "But Seana is generous with her offerings, I think."

Gavin's brows collided, remembering all the cats surrounding the potstill. It couldn't be that she had spied Seana at work. No. It was ridiculous to think she might have been a cat ... sitting there, watching in the shadows of the forest. "How would you know?" he asked casually, exploring her eyes. They were so deep a green that it made a mon think of a rich, cool glade. But they weren't cat eyes, not at all.

Cat grinned up at him, her toes curling again. "The grass around her potstill is quite consumed!"

"Aha!" Gavin allowed. It was true; not a bluidy thing grew about the potstill for at least a yard. He wondered idly what the *whiskie* must do to a mon's gut if it burned grass, but didn't say so.

"*Uisge beatha* has the power to heal, you know? 'Tis a gift from the gods, and only a few mortals have been charged to keep the ancient recipes. Seana is a verra special lady."

Gavin had never quite looked at Seana's *whiskie* through those eyes. "A gift from the Gods?" he repeated, looking down at the ground, nodding though he wasn't sure if he agreed.

"And you're a verra lucky mon if she shares her recipe with you," Cat added. "Seana must trust you verra much?"

"I did not say that," Gavin corrected her. "I merely said I would supply her with grain and that she would share the profits."

She seemed to think about that a moment and nodded. "Makes sense."

There was one last oatcake remaining, and Gavin pointed to it, offering it to her.

Her delicate brows twitched. "Are ye certain? You havena eaten much," she protested.

Gavin assured her, "I've had plenty lass, and your company is payment enough."

As he watched, her face lit from the inside. Her green eyes glittered fiercely and, suddenly compelled to, he reached out to wipe a bit of blue paint that remained upon her cheekbone—just a little smidgeon, not enough to really capture anyone's attention, unless one was inspecting every inch of her lovely face—which he was. Every time she turned away, he found himself studying every little thing—from her luscious mouth that had a natural upward curve, to her tiny little button nose.

She recoiled at first, and then realizing he only meant to wipe her face, she stilled, letting him rub the stain. "You're a guid mon," she offered suddenly. "If it please you, I would verra much like to help you finish building your home."

Gavin responded much too quickly, dropping his hands at once. "I don't need any help," he said defensively, and then regretted it, because her shoulders slumped and her smile faded by degrees. "But aye," he relented quickly, "if it please you, then you may help."

Her brilliant smile returned at once and she picked up the last oatcake, waving it before him one final time to give him a chance to protest. When he did not, she ate it slowly, savoring the delicious treat, and Gavin felt contented to the core of his being. Somehow, her presence comforted him, and if the truth be known, he found more pleasure in her company than he did in the building of his new home.

In fact, he found more pleasure simply talking with her than he had over anything in his life.

He didn't dare explore that fact too closely.

Together, they spent the remainder of the day working on his door, and by the gloaming, there was a fine, sturdy door in place.

"Where di' ye learn to do such work?" he asked.

She winked at him. "I was born knowin'."

Gavin frowned at her response.

After talking together nearly all the day long he still knew next to nothing about her.

"Ye've chosen a guid spot for your house," she said, as they stood back to admire the day's work.

Nestled against the bosom of the forest, the little house wasn't conspicuously out in the open, but neither was it so close to the trees that a good blaze might endanger the woodlands. And settled at the feet of *Chreagach Mhor*, it would escape the worst of the Highland winds. Up above, *Chreagach Mhor* rose against the afternoon sky, a majestic suzerain reigning over the landscape.

Cat examined the little house with arms crossed. "*Cailleach Bheur* smiles upon you," she offered.

Cailleach Bheur was the blue-faced mother of winter, who struck up mountains to shield living creatures from the bitter winds. Gavin peered up at the fortress above on the blufftop, its enormous tower silhouetted by the setting sun, and shuddered at the thought of the MacKinnon's first wife. After handing her husband their newborn bairn, she had flung herself from that tower window. Her death had escalated a thirty-year feud and forced all the neighboring clans to choose a side. Not surprisingly, they had all chosen the MacKinnon's. It was a joyous occasion that his new wife had now born him a new babe. At night, the grey tower, with its golden light in the high window, looked like a candle in the darkness—a guiding light.

"Do you believe in the old gods?" Gavin asked—as much out of curiosity as to appease his own lately wondering mind. When he'd first spied her, she had been wearing the woad of the painted ones—something no one, not even his grandsire had ever witnessed firsthand, for those people, like their stories, had long since faded from the memories of the living. Now it seemed they were nothing more than legend, except for the strange woman at his side.

Lowering her hands to her hips, she tilted him a questioning glance, her eyes studying him. And then she shrugged. "What does it matter what a mon believes, Gavin Mac Brodie... as long as he believes in something?"

Gavin blinked at her answer, taken aback by the simplicity of it.

"With faith there are no questions," she offered, "but without it there are no answers."

In one fell swoop, she had slain both his curiosity and his ambivalence.

He stood there looking at her, admiring her lovely face, her beauty completely undiminished by the dirt beneath her fingernails or the dirty smudges upon her high cheeks. "I was wondering about the woad, is all."

The green of her eyes glittered fiercely. "It is the way of my people," she offered, but her expression forbade him to ask any more.

Gavin sighed. It seemed he was destined to be left wanting, because short of tying her up and torturing her for answers, she didn't seem inclined to give any.

When the time came for Gavin to leave, he felt a keen disappointment, though it had little to do with having to leave his nearly completed house. He found he wasn't quite ready to leave Cat yet, though he knew he must. The woods were familiar but not so familiar that he was willing to go traipsing through the creeping mist at night.

Somehow knowing that she would not come along with him, and hoping to find a way to keep her around, Gavin offered her the use of his house. There was no reason for a good roof to go unused, he thought—especially when she had been the one to raise it.

Anyway, he was beginning to suspect that she had nowhere else to go, because she wasn't in much of a hurry to get there. This time he purposely left her with his dagger for protection, his tartan for warmth and all the food that remained in the sack.

Still he was reluctant to go.

For the longest moment, as she stood in the doorway of his new home, wrapped in his tartan, Gavin had the greatest sense of longing... to reach out ... touch her.

Something in her eyes invited him... and yet... he didn't quite trust himself—nor did he truly know what was expected. He only knew that his body ached and that if given half a chance, he would love to feel the sweet warmth of her flower open to embrace him.

Swallowing hard, he left her, though reluctantly, tearing himself away. He turned his back to her and bade his legs to move toward the forest, looking back only once... but it was his undoing, because in the twilight, she looked like a dream... a lovely chimera that would vanish with but a whisper of wind.

She waved, and he turned and made himself go, praying that she would still be there in the morn.

He decided that tonight he would tell his brothers that he intended to move out. Who knew where Cat might go once he occupied the little house. But mayhap if she were agreeable, he would help her find shelter amidst his kin. With that in mind, he made his way home, seeing the woods in a whole new light.

As the fireflies lit to guide his way, and the cats all blinked as he passed, he thought about the will-o'-the-wisp. Mayhap, just mayhap, there truly was magik out there.

If so, Cat was surely one of the fair folk, for there was a light in her eyes he had never spied before, and he sighed at the thought of seeing those beautiful green jewels on the morrow.

For the second time in just a few days, he whistled and sang all the way home.

CHAPTER 5

Just a sliver of moonlight peeked through the thick mist outside. The tower window remained open for the moment, but the nights were growing colder now, and the air no longer held any warmth beyond the gloaming.

Glenna, the midwife, appeared in the doorway of their bedchamber, looking quite fierce, though Iain MacKinnon had eyes only for his wife and his new daughter. Seated at Page's bedside, her husband coddled the babe, smiling down into her face and rubbing his knuckles reverently over the tiny cheek bones.

"She has your nose, I think," Page offered, waving Glenna into the room.

"Dinna say so!" Iain returned, sounding affronted, his brows colliding. "I see only you in this sweet child!"

Page was hardly in the frame of mind to argue, but she definitely saw Iain's nose and the babe's eyes were his as well —sunlit amber.

"When you two doves are done cooing, we've had a wee visit from *Bodachan Sabhaill*," Glenna complained.

When his wife screwed her face, Iain explained. "A haunting in the barn."

"We're missing a palette full of new candles!" Glenna railed. "Och, but damn! But we spent all day shaping those tapers and then we laid them all out flat to harden, and now they are gone—every last one!"

"Give the remaining candles to our guests," Iain said pleasantly. "We can use the pitch in here, dinna worry Glenna."

Glenna would not budge from the doorway. "Nay! Not with the babe!" she declared. "The smoke will blacken her lungs!"

Both Iain and Page peered up at her, smiling gently at the exaggeration. Certainly this child would find herself protected and spoiled by every member of this clan, of that there was little doubt—most particularly by her older brother, who was abed early now after having spent literally all day long at the babe's bedside—guarding her, he'd claimed, from the Sassenach hordes. No doubt he was still feeling a little insecure after his own ordeal with David, despite that Iain had reassured him no one would steal the babe away. Poor boy had nearly fallen asleep standing up and Glenna had whisked him away to a proper bed.

Glenna grumbled beneath her breath. "Why waste the best of our stores on that Sassenach loving wastrel?"

The wastrel in question was none other than King David of Scotia and Iain and Page shared an amused glance. Apparently, their eldest son wasn't the only one with an axe to grind.

"Give David the remaining candles," Iain demanded to Glenna's dismay.

The light in the chamber seemed to darken with her expression, almost as though she had willed it. Though in fact, the remaining candles were burnt to nubs, drowning their wicks in their wax.

"We can make do until they are gone, and in the meantime, you can make some more," Iain suggested. He gave Page a wink that twinkled full of love.

Glenna sighed. "And when will that be, prithee? Those ne'er-do-wells have been here more than a week now with no sign of the lass. When will they go away?"

"When they are certain she has fled the area," Iain suggested. "Apparently, David hopes to wed her to an English lord to appease her brother, though the lass seems reluctant."

Page laughed softly. "To say the least!"

"For shame!" Glenna berated. "How can ye harbor that odious man after he once did the same to you—thieving your son as he did. I dinna care one whit that he seems to believe 'tis for the guid of all. Who gave him the bluidy right?"

"He is a legal claimant to the throne," Iain reasoned.

"Humph! And so are you!" she returned, stomping a foot. "So is your son for that matter! And so is my fist," she said, raising it for both Page and Iain to see.

Page laughed, though she knew this discussion would only incite tempers. At the moment, Iain was enraptured with the babe, but she knew Glenna would not leave off until her husband's ire was finally pricked. "'Tis not the same," Page offered.

"Isn't it?" was all Glenna said in response, and her hands went again to her hips.

"Let us not dwell upon the past," Iain charged, smiling largely at the babe. "Not in the presence of so much hope." He tickled the babe's chin with his lips.

"Verra well," Glenna relented. "But I willna like it!" she declared, and stormed away.

Iain rose from the chair, never looking toward the door. He spilled their daughter into Page's arms with a warm smile, and said, "I love you, my dear wife. And she looks *exactly* like you."

Page only smiled, thinking that her husband was stubborn and blind, but alas, he was blind with love for her, and for the first time in her life, she understood the power of such a devotion.

She watched him as he made his way to one of the diminishing tapers, lifting up the candle along with its holder. He carried it to the pitch torch, and then removed the taper from the holder, setting the flame to the pitch. It flared at once, brightening the room with a dirty orange glow.

"When do you think he will leave?" Page ventured, admiring the wide set of her husband's shoulders.

Iain turned to her, pin-points of flame reflected in his deep amber eyes. "Soon, I hope, lest I run out of good will. God's breath but he does engender so much ill will."

Page sobered at that, and said honestly, "'Tis because he seems quite unconcerned about who he suppresses in the name of peace." She rocked the babe in her arms, shuddering softly over the memory of what they had done to Iain's son. The poor child had not spoken for months after they had taken him from his father, but she did not dare remind her husband of that. Still, she had to ask, "Are ye certain you trust him this time?"

Iain blew out the taper and set it back in the holder. He placed both upon a table and then went to the window, closing the shutters before returning to the bedside. His smile faded, and in the devilish light, Page could easily forget that he was her soft-hearted husband. In the orange glow of the torch light, his eyes were shadowed as he looked down upon their child in her arms. There was no need to speak a word for she knew instinctively what he was thinking.

"Trust has nothing to do with aught," he told her. "King or nay, if David betrays me again, I will carve out his heart and

I'm certain he knows it. Though just to be certain, you shall remain here... safe in our chamber... and you, the babe and my son will keep a guard at all times."

❧

AS PLANNED, GAVIN BROKE THE NEWS OF HIS IMMINENT departure to his brothers. No one seemed the least bit surprised, and neither were they disappointed.

Clearly, the current arrangement was equally disconcerting to them all, though they did put up a token of a protest, reassuring him that the manor would always be his home—particularly during the long winters, when the chill winds seeped into every fiber of a mon's bones.

He'd been just about to tell them about Cat too, but, for some reason, he kept that bit of information to himself—mayhap so they wouldn't feel like he was letting them off the hook so easily. Cat's presence at the house was temporary anyway, and the winters indeed would grow long and cold. By then, surely Seana's haggis would have improved by much and it comforted him to know he had a place to go.

Although he wasn't yet prepared to haul everything he owned out to the little house, he carted out a few supplies, and when he arrived, he found himself surprised yet again.

He wandered into the new house to find that Cat had built a small pit in the center of the room using stones. Peering up, he saw that she had allowed for the smoke's escape through a small aperture in the ceiling. It was so skillfully done that he hadn't noticed it before now.

There were a number of half-burned unlit tapers in the room and the house smelled like beeswax candles and had the look of a cozy little hovel, even devoid of furniture as it was still. Once he brought his bed and built a few small conveniences, he would nearly be set.

He didn't ask her where the supplies had come from. If there was any magik at work here, he didn't care.

"In the winter, you can place your kindling against the walls," she said. "It'll help keep the chill at bay." He could see that she had constructed something like braces to keep piles of kindling secure against the walls.

It was genius, of course, to have a double wall for insulation, though Gavin wasn't particularly pleased to see that she was working her fingers to the bone—she must be; all this work didn't magically happen.

Not to mention the fact that he had never met a woman who did men's work better than men did—far better than he did. He scratched his head, "Och, lass... I have no way to repay you for all this."

She smiled benevolently. "As you have said so eloquently... the gift of your company is quite enough, Gavin Mac Brodie."

And so he had. And so it was. For his part, he was simply pleased to see that she had decided to remain for a few days.

As for the matter of locating water, Cat fashioned a divining rod, and then set out to pace the area while Gavin followed behind her, wondering how the devil she was going to discover well water without actually digging. In truth, he had heard of such a thing from his Grandminny Fia, but had never actually seen anyone do it.

By early afternoon, she had divined a spot, bidding him to trust her, and Gavin did. Setting aside his doubts, he began to dig. He dug all day, and well into the next, and the next, not allowing Cat to help at all with this task—well, because, damn it, he was a man, and a man must do his part.

He made her watch—and eat, since she seemed to like to do that—until his hole was deep enough for a body to stand in. All the while, she sat there above him, her legs dangling into the pit, chatting endlessly—an easy banter that he suspected hid more than it revealed.

On the other hand, there were other things she seemed to have no qualms over revealing to him.

God help him, if he were any other man, he might have reached up at any given moment and slid his thumb easily across those lovely bits.

Even more appealing—damn his lusty soul—he could have buried his face between her thighs and drank from the well of her body.

His most rabid thirst right now had little to do with water.

Instead, he shoveled furiously, saying nothing, trying to look beyond the lovely legs she tempted him with and those dark red curls. The longer he shoveled, and the longer she sat, the more mischievous she seemed to become.

Gavin began to wonder if she were the devil himself come to tempt him.

Cat knew full well what she was doing.

Not that she had ever lain with a man before, but her people were not pietists. They loved where they wished. And right now, though it would surely confuse matters, she wanted Gavin Mac Brodie.

The sight of him working so furiously down there in his pit—bare backed—made her smile. She had never seen a man work so desperately just to keep from taking his pleasures—and she knew full well that's what was on his mind. She recognized the sparkle of lust in his dark green eyes and the surreptitious glances he cast between her thighs were hardly lost to her.

But neither were the glimpses she offered him any accident.

She had been drawn to him from the instant she had met him. In truth, had she not been she would have been long gone by now, especially knowing they were still searching for her.

But for some reason she still couldn't go.

She had convinced herself that if she fled north, they would surely anticipate that move, and overtake her quickly if she were on foot. And that was probably true, so she had intended to steal herself a horse. But the simple fact was that now she didn't want to go.

His pit was growing deeper and deeper and soon she would be out of his reach. She had hoped, desperately, that he would reach out for her—och, but he was nothing like the groping fools she had known.

He was a sweet, gentle man with the face of an angel and a body that stole her breath.

"Don't ye need a break by now?" she asked.

"Nay!" He refused to look up at her and Cat giggled softly. "I'm not tired," he persisted.

She scooted around the edge of the pit so that he had no choice but to acknowledge her, and crossed her legs, knowing full well that his view was quite telling from down there. "Aren't ye hungry at all?" she asked him as seductively as she knew how.

He paused suddenly, leaning on his shovel, and peered up at her, swallowing as his eyes lit upon the moon of her arse... and the other secrets displayed for his eyes alone. He licked his lips and Cat felt like leaping down into the pit and kissing him ferociously. Soon, she would have no choice but to leave and she didn't want to go before thanking Gavin the way she really wanted to.

"Och, lass," he said, and leaned upon the far wall of his pit, as though he were trying to put more distance between himself and the temptation she offered.

Cat sighed. She knew he was curious about where she was

from, but she wasn't ready to reveal herself yet—perhaps in part because she might then be compelled to actually go home —particularly if he found out who her brother was—Aidan, last of the blood of Aed, grandson of Donald MacAlpin, brother to Kenneth and the last of the Kings of Dal Riata.

After Aed's death, her kinsmen had fled to the Mounth and there they remained. They kept mostly to themselves and had no love for politics, though as a distant claimant to the throne, David apparently perceived Aidan as a threat. He seemed to believe that with Cat in hand, her brother would never challenge him.

But he didn't know her brother.

Aidan wanted no part of Scotia, but provoking him was like poking a sleeping dragon.

If Gavin learned the truth, would he turn her over to the English lackey, or would he take her home himself?

Cat would rather die than end as the wife of a Sassenach.

She slid as far to the edge of the pit as was physically possible, peering down into the hole. "Verra nice," she declared.

A few loose bits of soil fell from the edge beneath her rear and she suddenly had an idea.

"But there's no water," he complained.

She grinned. "Not yet."

CHAPTER 6

Gavin couldn't even see out of the pit any longer, but it seemed to him that the shores of the loch across the way must surely be higher than he was at this point, and he told her so. "There's no water here," he announced, thinking how foolish it was to believe they would strike well water in the first spot he had cast his spade—whether or not she had bade him to believe it.

"Oh ye of little faith," she said.

Gavin lifted a brow at hearing that phrase so familiar from his scripture. "Where did ye hear that, lass?"

"Hear what?"

She scooted to the very edge of the pit and a cascade of soil spilled down the pit wall onto his feet. He frowned. "What you just said."

She arched a brow. "Well, I heard it from me, ye daft mon because I only now just said it. Didna ye hear me speak the words?" She grinned at him then, letting him know with her impish smile that she meant no harm.

"Never mind," Gavin groused, disconcerted that not once but twice now she had alluded to his lack of faith.

Was it true?

Had he lost his way?

How would she know, anyway? She was a pagan, painting herself with woad. In fact, perchance, just perchance she was, in fact, a faerie or a brownie—or one of those other annoying spirits.

Except that she wasn't annoying in the least.

She was, in fact, the most pleasant person he ever didn't really know—particularly for someone who seemed to have no home, no clothes and who hadn't eaten in so long that she had forgotten all semblance of manners.

He still didn't know a damned thing about her and that fact soured his mood with every stab of his spade.

If she left him, how would he find her? He didn't have the first notion even where she'd come from!

For the past few days, he had felt far more alive than he had in an age, and he didn't want this feeling to end.

It was like being drunk on Seana's brew, except that he hadn't touched a drop.

He just suddenly felt ...

Love, Gavin Mac Brodie, he heard Seana say again. *If love is not some form of magik, then I dunno what is.*

Gavin peered up at Cat, wondering... was it possible to lose his heart so quickly without even realizing? Didn't two people have to *agree* to love one another?

He thought about his sister Meggie, and how the Sassenach had simply stolen her away. He was pretty sure Meggie would have put up a good fight. And yet there she was ... lovin' that Sassenach anyway.

And Colin? His brother surely would never have gone looking for love. And yet it had found him nevertheless.

As for Leith, apparently, Leith had always loved Alison, though he had somehow kept that fact to himself.

Confused by it all, Gavin started shoveling again, and Cat

held her foot out, giggling as she teased him with those adorable toes. Och, but he had a mind to bite them—not hard, but just enough to show her how dangerous it was to tease a grown man—particularly one who was weak as he was. And he was most definitely weak; it was all he could do to keep his mind on his work.

"Ye're going to fall," he warned.

"Not me," she swore, and then she perched herself even more precariously upon the edge.

Suddenly, she gasped and fell right into the pit atop him, knocking him backward, straddling him as he fell against the wall. He pushed the spade aside, not wanting it to hurt her. She settled squarely on his belly, her sweet damp bits hot against his skin and his heart vaulted into his throat.

She gifted him with a throaty laugh and he swallowed convulsively as she wrapped her lean limbs about his waist.

Her lovely lips curved wickedly. "You saved me," she declared.

Gavin barely shook his head—barely able to. "There wasna much danger," he reassured her, swallowing hard. "Ye fell but just a few feet."

Gavin's heart beat faster. His blood simmered as he gauged her reaction to him.

He was hardly unaffected, and his body felt alive with a will of its own.

He knew she knew it too and her smile hitched a notch higher, the curve of it sensual and impish.

Gavin swallowed. "Och, but ye have strong legs," he offered weakly, feeling the nob rise in his throat.

And that's not all that was rising.

His hands grew moist while his mouth grew parched.

Gavin felt a shock of pleasure as her hand splayed across the skin of his chest. His body hardened completely as her fingers skipped across his nipples.

"Och, lass," he protested, but whatever he was about to say died in his throat as she leaned to place her lips to his bare skin—a hot, wet kiss that made Gavin dizzy.

She peered up at him, smiling mischievously and his heart hammered fiercely.

"You dinna know what you are doing to me," he warned.

She nodded slowly, her eyes teasing. "Oh, but I do," she said, and squeezed her legs about his waist again, pressing her private flesh against his belly.

Gavin fought another wave of dizziness. All his blood floated into his head—well, not all of it, God save him!

Her hands disappeared at her back and she worked loose his breacan from his belt, pulling it aside and yanking it from between them, leaving Gavin completely without protection against her eyes and her wiles.

If she reached back, just a little bit behind her, she'd find a pole as hard as the handle of his spade.

She suddenly scooted back, brushing his erection with the crack of her arse, lifting up her—his—green tunic, and nestling his heat against her soft, hot flesh.

Gavin felt suddenly as though he had a fever. His skin was on fire. His blood burned.

To join their bodies, all he would have to do right now is lift her up, and move her back... just a wee bit... and place her gently upon his cock. The pit was small enough that he could brace his legs against one side and his shoulders against the other and let her ride him of her own accord.

Sweat beaded upon his brow.

His heartbeat roared in his ears and his blood sang through his veins.

For a moment, they both simply stared at one another.

Cat held her breath, recognizing the desire in his eyes, compelled by it, excited by it. It was exactly what she had hoped for, but seeing it now left her weak. Her heart beat furiously against her ribs and she lapped at lips gone suddenly dry.

There was something about Gavin Mac Brodie that sang to her heart—something that she had never felt with any other man.

He looked at her as though she were perfect.

She liked that feeling... she liked everything he made her feel... every shiver of her skin... ever tingle of her flesh... every word that came out of his mouth.

And right now, she wanted nothing more than to feel him deep inside her. This was what she had saved herself for... this very moment. Every kiss she had ever denied, every touch she had forestalled... it was because she had been seeking this incredible feeling.

And to think she had discovered it in the most unexpected of places—in the arms of a Scoti stranger.

He opened his mouth—to protest, she knew, but she didn't want to hear it. She lifted her finger to his lips.

Swallowing a little, Cat nipped her lip and scooted backward, bending so that her arse lifted as she moved to kiss him.

It was awkward at first, their lips touching gently as she lifted herself over his manhood and touched her most private lips to his hot, erect flesh. At the same time, she parted her mouth and he sent his tongue on a timid foray. A shock of pleasure sidled through her at the intimate caress, the coupling of their mouths.

Cat accepted him, sucking in a shaky breath as she lapped his tongue and without thinking much about it, without allowing herself to hesitate, she slid herself over his shaft, bearing down upon him.

He shuddered violently, groaning fiercely, and so did she, as their bodies fused as one.

Gavin groaned deep in the back of his throat, feeling such an ecstasy as he had never felt in all his life—not even that first time as a virgin had he felt such a rush of blood into his head.

She whimpered and that was all it took.

The shovel forgotten, the pit neglected—not caring where they were, their bodies began to move together in the most delicious accord. She rode him gently, without hurry, her body tightening about his shaft, milking him sweetly.

Sweating, covered in grime, but unmindful of it, they kissed each other's bodies. He laved her breasts with his tongue, tasting the salt of her skin, suckling her nipples, worshiping her body.

His feet searched for firmer support, finding purchase on the flat end of his spade, kicking it into the soil beneath him as she moved against his body in wild abandon.

Och, God, but she was lovely.

Every touch she gave was pure magik.

She must be magik.

Moving together in a dance as old as time, they moved together until Gavin felt her body convulse around him and it sent wave after wave of undeniable pleasure shooting through him. He cried out, spilling his seed deep within her womb.

It was only when they both stopped moving at last, and she lay spent upon his bare chest, their bodies moist from exertion, that he realized he was suddenly ankle deep in water.

He blinked.

"Christ!" he exclaimed—but not just because he had ventured to heaven and back in her arms.

They'd struck water.

The well was filling with water.

CHAPTER 7

Unlike that first time so long ago, there was not an ounce of regret. Gavin felt only euphoria.

Laughing, he kissed Cat soundly upon the lips, shuddering again.

Three strange words fought to emerge upon his tongue, but they startled him and he held back.

Her smile was so full of joy and her eyes fairly sparkled. Her cheeks were flushed and lovely. "I told ye tae have a bit o' faith, didn't I?"

Gavin laughed again, lifting her up as the well filled to his shins.

"Damn!" he exclaimed. "You're a witch forsooth!" he announced, though he said it with the biggest smile he could muster.

She'd found water.

Magik!

Aye, the lass was magik pure and simple.

Because more than having somehow found his water without much effort, she'd tapped another well that he'd thought long since run dry.

Faith, she'd said.

Aye, he was going to have a wee bit o' faith—faith that she had been sent to him just when he needed her. Faith that she was exactly what he needed.

Laughing together, he helped her up out of the well, patting her firm round bottom after he pushed her up and out of the pit. And then she helped him up, filthy and muddy as he was.

❧

COLIN FINISHED REPAIRING HIS SECTION OF WALL, AND then he and Leith began to shore up the rest of the building.

"When the bastard said he was leavin', apparently he meant *right now*," Leith complained.

Gavin hadn't been about for two days now. He'd left with one of the carts and had yet to return—not to sleep, to eat or to say "go to hell and take your bluidy wall wi' ye!"

Colin didn't have much to say about that. Gavin was the one Brodie who was a slave to duty and conscience. That he had taken a rare moment to do what he pleased was a good thing, as far as Colin was concerned and Colin applauded him for it—even if it left the rest of them with a little more work to do.

Anyway, if he was truly moving away to No Mon's Land, they would not see him every day as it was. It was about time they learned to do without him.

Though he and Gavin rarely shared confidences, he thought he understood what was ailing his little brother. Were their roles reversed, he didn't think he could stand to be around so much lip smacking and cooing either—especially when he had been alone most of his life.

Nay, Colin begrudged Gavin nothing.

"I wish he would at least return the cart," Leith groused.

And then he stood, scratching his head. "Ha'e ye seen the lumber for the roof?"

Colin shook his head. He reached up to swipe a rivulet of sweat from his brow. "I've not seen it since two weeks past when we set it aside to work on the walls."

Leith tossed down his hammer. "Damn thievin' folk around here!" He cast Colin a questioning glance. "Do ye think Montgomerie would be up to his auld tricks?"

Colin laughed. "Nay, Meggie would have his arse," he assured Leith. But then he wondered. It wasn't like Gavin to take anything that wasn't specifically assigned to him, but could his brother be so damned desperate to be away from them that he would have *borrowed* their lumber to finish his roof?

But nay... he would never. Gavin was the most honest fellow Colin had ever known—despite being his brother.

Leith apparently had the same thought. "The pinions are gone, too," he said. "Mayhap it's time we paid a visit to our little brother's new home?"

ALTHOUGH GAVIN HAD SPENT MOST OF HIS LIFE CELIBATE, he'd made up for every lost moment during the past two days. He and Cat made love again in the meadow once they'd hauled themselves out of the well. And then again in the loch after making the trek across the field.

They enjoyed the privacy of his home, pleasuring each other's bodies by the firelight until the break of dawn.

Truth to tell, until now, in Cat's arms, he had never realized what it truly meant to have a home, for it didn't matter where they were, when they were together, it was exactly the right place to be.

The well was half full now, and a few good rains would fill it completely.

The house was completed and he considered now whether to bring his bed from the manor or to build a new one. He felt perhaps it was time for all things new, and he wondered what sort of bed Cat would like.

While he took his axe to the trees, she sat mixing some sort of tincture for the cut he'd sustained on his foot from the lip of the spade. It made him blush to remember that he'd pressed his heel so hard into the metal that it had cut into his flesh—and more, that he'd never even noticed until much later.

Only one thing troubled him. He was getting used to the lass. And now, though he didn't believe in any sort of magik, he was beginning to fear even the possibility.

What if she wasn't here to stay?

What if he wasn't enough to keep her?

What if he awoke one morning to find her gone?

He might be a man in truth, but he thought he would weep like a wee bitty bairn for the rest of his given days.

CHAPTER 8

South was not his favorite way to ride.

Aidan sniffed the air about him. The scattered forests still held their verdant green, the ferns remained full, with new growth unfurled. Spear thistle and primrose were still in bloom and the scent of heather was strong in the air. There should be moorland nearby; his nose never lied.

He surveyed his surroundings, thinking that *Cailleach Bheur* was not so kind to these folk, leaving them vulnerable to the sting of winter winds despite that they were far enough north that cold remained their bedfellow. The mother of winter had sheltered his own people for ages now, coddling them like tiny babes in her warm bosom, throwing up mounts to discourage more timid men from venturing into their crib.

Though his people needed no king, Aidan was as close as any north man came to such a title. He led with his heart, and protected his kinsmen with every fiber of his soul. His father had done the same before him, and had died with the sword of one of these Sassenach loving Scoti in his belly. His mother too had died defending their home, leaving him to raise a brood of five—his favorite being his sister Cat. That bastard would-be king of Scotia had stolen her directly from her bower.

If they took her far enough south she would be lost to them forever. And if she returned north with a Sassenach in her belly she need not return at all.

For two centuries his people had remained inconspicuous and stayed out of men's politics, and as much as it would pain him he would not allow a Sassenach into their midst—not even one whose blood ran through his veins. In truth, he shared the blood of many, including David of Scotia... but that did not make them the same.

Riding with the wind, he'd brought twenty warriors to search for Catrìona, and hoped they would find her before it was too late. The thought of passing a winter without her bonny smile filled his heart with a bitter black melancholia. Nor did he relish the thought of losing a single man or woman, as few of their kindred that remained.

"The Scoti king is near," his scout said, returning from his reconnaissance. "They search these woodlands for Cat, though it appears she evades them still."

Aidan smiled thinly.

Catrìona would know what to do. His sister was a warrior, after all. He had trained her well. He had raised the lass since her very first smile and she could wield that as adeptly as she could a blade.

All of his people were warriors for in the Mounth it was a matter of life and death.

"Continue searching here," Aidan directed his men. He'd brought his most fearsome warriors—all of them willing to die for every woman and child in their care. That was the way they had survived all this time, leaving no man to himself.

Painted in the woad of their ancestors—a reminder to them all of where they had come from—they rode white steeds—ghost horses, trained to step lightly and travel, not with haste, but with precision. To race through the Mounth was a death sentence. They took their cues from mother earth, listening to the secrets she had to whisper, and they missed nothing—not so much as a child's weightless footstep on solid rock, nor a single broken twig.

They were the last of the painted ones, and they carried the heartbeats of their ancestors in their blood, and the song of their people in their hearts.

"Ride," he commanded his men. "Turn every stone until she is found!"

❧

AS COOL AS THE WEATHER REMAINED HIGH IN THESE HILLS, the heather bloomed a brilliant violet against a vivid carpet of green. While Gavin lay upon his back in a bed of yellow buttercups, Cat knelt at his feet with a bowl of her healing potion in her hands, slathering the blue concoction upon the bottom of his foot.

"I canna see as how your war paint will heal my foot—anyway, it doesna hurt," he reassured her.

"*This*—" She held up the bowl. "—is *not* war paint," she reprimanded him. "And though 'tis blue, it is *not* the same as the paint you found me wearing. However," she enlightened him. "*That* is not war paint either."

He winked at her. "Whatever it is, I'd like to see ye wear it often—and only that."

She laughed softly. "It is a tribute to my ancestors—to yours, too, Gavin Mac Brodie, for we share the same forefathers."

"Forsooth, I ha'e never met a blue person in all my days," Gavin swore. "As far as I can tell, none of my kin ever painted themselves either. Alas, I do not share your pixie blood."

"Pixie!" she protested, pretending to be affronted. By his grin, she knew he was teasing.

"Aye, judging by your height," he said. "Pixie or faerie, one —I swear your minge is magic!"

Cat slapped his leg, but laughed nevertheless. "Stay still, Gavin, or I will surely put a hex on you!" she threatened.

"You already have!" he told her, and dipped his toe into her bowl, then slathered the tincture across her face with his foot.

It took her completely by surprise. He had been such a grouch at first but now his mood had lightened considerably. No longer did he brood, and she concluded that he must have needed to appease his willy. It made sense to her. A man could simply not go his entire life without a little love—and he had, she was certain because he'd had that pinched look about him of a man whose bollocks were petrified from lack of use.

A grin broke across her face. "Why you!" And she took her paint and crawled between his knees, lying atop his chest to swipe it across his face.

"Och, but ye're a pawky wench," he swore, and leapt up to take the bowl from her hands.

"Nay!" she shrieked, and then the two of them began to tussle over the bowl, dipping in their fingers and slathering it on each other wherever they could reach.

Cat giggled profusely as they rolled along the meadow together, leaving blue stains upon the buttercups as they passed.

Soon they would have to have a very long talk, and she would need to tell him everything, but not right now—right now, she was enjoying the moment, wanting it never to end.

And feeling particularly wicked, she threw off her tunic and began to paint her breasts with the tincture, drawing in the style of her people.

The look in his eyes turned sober then. His blond brows arched and his green eyes gleamed, and then he pinned her down and lay her upon the grass to make love to her yet again.

Seana anticipated that her husband was becoming vexed, so she made an excuse about checking the potstill and ventured that way to check on Gavin.

She found the brew nearly ready and smiled, patting the potstill's copper belly. Her Da would have been pleased with this batch. A black cat rushed toward her, fanning its tail across her shins, and she smiled down at the creature, bending to lift it into her arms. "My Love," she cooed. "Where is papa today?"

The cat gave her a little plaintive "mech" that made her laugh—why she had no idea. It was just a silly cat sound, but she liked to think she understood exactly what was meant.

For the moment, she relished the feel of her little feline companion, and looked about to inspect all the furry friends the cat had gathered about the potstill.

Near a particularly fat fern, another black cat rolled over on its back and she set My Love down and sauntered over to rub this one's belly as it seemed to enjoy. And then, reluctantly, she let them all be and made her way toward Gavin's new home at the edge of the woods.

She couldn't wait to see how much progress he had made, and a part of her was quite pleased that he would be around to guard her potstill all the way out here.

Besides, she understood perfectly why Gavin needed to establish himself as the master of his own home. She only hoped that he...

She froze as she broke through the tree line.

Two lovers cavorted in a bed of yellow buttercups alongside Gavin's new house. She blinked, not believing her eyes. And then, cheeks ablaze, she suddenly turned and fled before anyone could spy her standing there in the shade of the trees.

CHAPTER 9

"I swear 'tis true!" Seana told Meghan. She had run straight to the Montgomerie clearing and stood now talking to Gavin's sister in the courtyard.

Meghan's brows rose. "Gavin?" she asked, aghast. She pointed to her breast. "*My* brother, Gavin?"

"Och!" Seana exclaimed. "I know no other Gavins! Aye, I saw him—I swear it upon my father's *uisge beatha*!"

Meghan's expression suddenly turned fearful. "Oh, but no!" she said. "I heard my husband say that King David searches for a runaway prisoner. Do you think it could be her?"

Seana lifted her shoulders. "All I know is that your brother has found himself a lover!"

"And you're absolutely certain they are lovers?"

"Oh, yes!" Seana said, and her cheeks heated at once. "As certain as I can be!"

"Well, I'll bedamned," Meghan said, and she began to giggle nervously. "I truly never thought I'd see the day."

"The day for what?" her husband inquired, coming up

behind her and wrapping his arms about her waist. He gave her a little peck upon the cheek.

Meghan turned to face him, looking suddenly pained. Clearly she didn't want to lie to her husband but neither did she wish to betray her brother.

If in fact this was the same woman they were seeking, what would that mean for Gavin?

But she couldn't lie to her husband. She told him everything Seana had just revealed. And then Seana corroborated what she had seen.

Piers made a face that clearly betrayed his thoughts. This was yet another embroilment he would have to finagle their way out of, and unfortunately, there was only one way to do that; he must find the girl before anyone else found her.

❧

IAIN WAS HARDLY PLEASED TO BE LEAVING HIS WIFE AND newborn babe in order to search for some strange wench merely to serve David's political games.

Fresh in his mind was his ordeal with his own son and though David claimed he had not been a party to the deceit, the fact was that he had been the one to take his son across the border without ever having spoken to Iain, and it sat like a stone in his belly.

It stank of a lie.

And yet, David had stood behind Iain when he had defied Page's father's demands to return his daughter. Good thing, because it would be a cold day in Hell before Iain e'er relinquished the love of his life.

Riding beside the King of Scotia this late afternoon, his heart was only halfway in the search, and so he missed it when one of David's men spotted the lovers carousing in the meadow where Gavin Mac Brodie claimed he was building his new house. But having spied them, a chill raced down Iain's spine, for he knew instinctively that this could lead to yet another feud. They were not so far from recent hostilities that a single ordeal would not put the clans at odds again.

"Christ," he said, and followed David and his men down the bluff, taking the rocky path down. At the juncture before the forest, they were met by Leith and Colin Mac Brodie emerging from the woods.

All three men eyed one another curiously, and then, without warning, Piers de Montgomerie and his band of men appeared on the narrow road coming from his clearing.

"Thank God!" David declared, and spurred his mount toward Piers, evidently pleased to find himself among new allies.

"What goes here?" Leith asked.

Broc urged his mount forward. "We seek a runaway," he explained to Leith and to Colin, eyeing them both meaningfully.

"She's a rebel," David said, returning with Piers at his heels. "Potentially, a traitor to the crown!"

Iain's mount pranced anxiously beneath him, sensing his tension. "Which crown is that?" he asked darkly.

Though he had no designs on any crown, for David to announce such a thing before his face was crude, to say the least. By most Highlanders' opinions, Iain had more right to the throne than David, for David had spent the whole of his life suckling the teat of a Sassenach maid. He had spent his youth as a ward of the English court and had brought north the seeds of English deceit.

"The *rightful* crown of Scotia," David replied arrogantly. "The *only* crown," he maintained.

Iain tightened his grip on the reins, a muscle ticking at his jaw, but said nothing, knowing that if he but spoke the word, his simple declaration would part the sea of Scotia's loyalties. Luckily for David, he had no interest in politics or kinslaying.

"At any rate, we've tracked the girl to this hovel beneath the bluffside," David explained to Piers and the Brodie brothers. "We have no quarrel with any, save for the man who abets her now."

Leith's expression turned menacing. "If you speak of that house yonder, it belongs to my brother Gavin. Gavin keeps no women," he assured David.

"Nay?" David countered, his tone belligerent.

"We saw them together," Broc interjected solemnly. "They have gone inside."

For a moment, the leaders of the three present clans, Leith, Piers and the MacKinnon all shared looks. David inched his mount toward Piers, a taciturn message.

If they were to do battle here, right now, David had five men at his beck and call. Piers had four. Iain had only brought Broc. Leith and Colin were alone. Nine against four... unless Piers forsook his liege.

Iain watched every small move, reading their body language, ready to draw his sword.

"Well, then," Colin offered, looking directly at David. "Let us go and speak to Gavin, but do him injury, and I will kill you myself, king or nay."

"*Diabhul!*" Catrìona cursed. She peered out between the shutters to spy the band of riders congregating where the road from the nearby farm ended, meeting woodland and heath.

"What is it?" Gavin asked.

She nibbled her fingers, stabbing her canine teeth into her cuticles with sudden fear.

They had discovered her.

What to do, what to do?

"Cat?" Gavin was warming water in a small kettle over the fire for a sponge bath as they were both covered from head to heels in the medicinal tincture she had made for his wound.

He left the kettle and moved to the window behind her, and she realized that time had run out to tell him the truth. Now, she must trust him to do the right thing.

Would he turn her over to King David?

Or would he fight for her?

She cringed at the thought of the latter, for as much as she loathed the thought of ending as some fat Sassenach's bride, neither did she want Gavin to die trying to defend her. She feared she loved him.

Aye, but she did.

She loved him as surely as she breathed.

Gavin peered out from the window. "It looks like my brothers," he said, his tone rife with curiosity. "...and my sister's husband." He gave her a confused look and Cat immediately went to snatch up the tunic he had given her to put it on before they could discover her naked again.

Gavin too gathered his clothing and he quickly donned the breacan, belting it faster than she had ever seen a man belt a breacan in all her life.

He took her by the hand and made to draw her out of the door, but she held back. She shook her head fearfully, refusing. His brows drew together in confusion, but he let her go.

"What is the meaning of this?" Gavin shouted, coming out of his house.

The riders all seemed to be in the middle of a heated discussion. Leith and Colin were the first to break away and come forward.

"You harbor a fugitive inside?" Leith asked without preamble.

Gavin screwed his face. "Fugitive?" He shook his head,

not understanding. "There is a girl within, aye, but she is no fugitive... she is..." He stumbled through an explanation, being uncertain of what she was, and wanting to call her his wife. Except that she wasn't, and his brothers knew that better than any. "She's..."

"I'll tell you what she is! She is my prisoner!" David exclaimed at once. He surged his mount forward, his hand ready upon the hilt of his sword. His men drew alongside him as though prepared to protect him.

A fight was surely brewing.

Gavin noticed that Montgomerie and his men kept their distance for the moment, watching the scene unfold, their stances unrevealing.

Now, Gavin thought, came the moment of truth. Would Montgomerie defy his liege for blood? Where did his true loyalties lie? With his sister and her kin? Or with his Sassenach loving puppet king?

Iain MacKinnon's horse sauntered forward, carrying its rider without much haste, every step assured by the body language of its master. "She was to become a ward of the English court," he said softly, though not timidly. His deep voice commanded respect, and instead of speaking over him, all voices quieted to hear what he would say. "Have you no knowledge of this?" he asked Gavin.

Gavin shook his head. "Nay, but the woman inside is under my protection," he told the MacKinnon. "I will not give her up without a fight."

The MacKinnon eyed him curiously. "So then have you given up your faith, preacher?"

Gavin shook his head again. "On the contrary," he argued. "I have only just found it, but that is neither here nor there. That woman inside is my bride!"

"Bride!" both Leith and Colin shouted at once.

"Bride?" Broc repeated, choking on the word.

Montgomerie's eyes widened incredulously. "Christ bedamned," he exclaimed, and spurred his mount, encircling the group of men, eyeing the new house as he went about, and particularly the roof. "Damn, this is a sturdy roof," he added offhand, complimenting Gavin in the oddest tone.

Gavin nodded, uncertain what to say, for he'd had no hand in building the damned roof. But then again he didn't want to admit that Cat had built it either. "Thank ye," he said belatedly, and then peered back at the door to see that Cat was peeking out through a crack, her liquid green eyes full of trepidation.

Anyway, he decided it was a damned peculiar thing to say with the trouble that was brewing.

As though only now noticing, Leith asked him, "Gavin... why the hell are you blue?"

"Because his *bride* is a damn savage!" David offered sourly, his words enraging Gavin.

Gavin leapt toward David, but Montgomerie maneuvered his horse between them, stopping him short.

"Enough of this banter!" David declared impatiently, and then shouted at the house. "Show yourself girl!"

Gavin moved back toward the door instinctively, ready to fight for the woman he loved.

Catrìona had known she could not hide forever.

The time had come to reveal herself.

She spied the men with King David—the ones who had stripped her and bound her, knowing that, if given the chance, they would do Gavin harm and she would not see him suffer for her sake.

Och, he had called her his bride.

She wanted to smile, but her throat thickened. She wished with all her heart that it were true.

A little timidly, she ventured out of the house, moving

toward Gavin, clinging to his back. He moved to shield her from the men's view, but she could still see beneath his arm pit.

Several of the men—all strangers to her—simply peered at one another curiously. One by one they all shared some silent message, their body language revealing something she knew instinctively.

Their wordless gestures bespoke a loyalty as old as time.

"Is it true?" one man asked. "Do you love her, brother?"

Gavin straightened his back, his arm snaking behind him to reach for her. "I do," he said without hesitation.

The man who had spoken conferred with another—a man who looked very much like Gavin, with his blond hair and wide-shouldered stance, save that his eyes were blue. The eldest of the two had called him brother.

Catrìona swallowed convulsively, knowing that these were the moments that would determine her fate.

Another man—the one who had complimented her roof—looked directly down at Cat, "Do you love him?" he demanded.

Catrìona nodded jerkily. Her legs trembled beneath her. Never had she been surrounded by so many strangers but she would not disgrace her brother or her kinfolk by cowering now before them. She squared her shoulders, realizing Gavin had not seen her gesture, and answered loudly for all to hear. "Aye, this man holds my heart!"

King David had yet to speak—not a word from the moment she had shown herself.

All at once, the crowd shifted, moving away from David. Horses surrounded her, entrapping her.

All she heard now were disembodied voices.

The deepest of them all—the one who had called Gavin a preacher—now asked David, "Is this the girl you seek, David?

Surely you have mistaken her?" he suggested with an undertone to his voice that held a certain menace. "After spending so much time in the English court, perhaps we savages all look alike?"

David said nothing.

And then Catrìona heard a voice that stopped her heart.

With twenty horsemen at his back, seven of them archers, Aidan rode boldly into their midst. He had watched until Catrìona appeared outside the door of the little hovel. He could never mistake his sister's brilliant mane of hair. It shone like copper under the glinting sun, even hidden as she was now behind so much horseflesh.

"Catrìona!" he shouted again.

He could see her rise on tippy toes, trying to peer over the barrier they had set between her and David's men. It was clear that David was outnumbered here and he gave a sign for his archers to put away their bows.

David's mount pranced nervously beneath him, but Aidan only gave him a cursory glance, recognizing the man he needed to speak with. He had not known what the MacKinnon would look like, but he recognized a true leader when he spied one.

"Iain MacKinnon," he shouted, "descendant of the sons of MacAlpin, I seek only thy council!"

The MacKinnon's horse spun to face him, and David stepped back, his face mottling, but despite his pack of soldiers on mules, he said nothing, and Aidan knew instinctively that he had been correct in his assumptions.

"I am Aidan," he revealed, looking away from David, meeting Iain's gaze, "last of the blood of Aed, grandson of Duncan MacAlpin, brother to Kenneth and the last of the Kings of Dal Riata."

The MacKinnon spurred his mount forward, his black

horse prancing with a confidence that its master obviously shared.

"I have no quarrel with you," Aidan was quick to say. "But the woman you hold is my sister. If you but return her to me now, we will take our leave and return to the Mounth."

The ensuing silence was deafening as both men assessed each other. After a moment, the MacKinnon peered behind him. "Is this true?" he asked at large.

It was Catrìona who stepped forward, weaving her way out of the protective horseflesh mantle they had cast about her. "Aye," she affirmed to the MacKinnon. "This man is, indeed, my brother."

"How is it you come to be so far from home?" the MacKinnon asked her.

Cat peered up at King David, who now suddenly seemed reluctant to speak a word. She weighed her own words wisely, sensing that she was surrounded by far too much male pride for anyone to leave unscathed if she but said the wrong word.

She held her head high, and lied through her teeth. "I went for a walk," she said and peered at her brother. She lifted a shoulder, a bit of a shrug.

Aidan lifted a single dark brow. Her brother was darker skinned than she, with hair that flowed down his back as black as sin. He was painted fiercely, dressed fully in war regalia, his black eyes shrewd.

He knew she sought to avoid bloodshed and he graciously allowed it.

The MacKinnon looked toward King David then. "What say you, David? You have yet to speak a word... is this the same woman you seek?"

David looked at her again, blinking, thwarted he realized.

She glanced at the one called Dùghall, the one she had

smacked on the forehead in order to escape. The man glared at her rudely, but said nothing, and in fact, averted his gaze.

It took David a long moment to finally reply. He inched his horse forward and pretended to look her over—a ruse, because he had been the one to order his men to strip her bare so that she would be less inclined to escape. And then he had ogled every inch of her though to his credit he had forbade his men to abuse her.

His horse pranced beneath him impatiently as he pretended to inspect her, and all the while the men formed a tighter band behind the MacKinnon laird—a move that was not lost to David.

It was clear to Cat in that moment where loyalties lay.

David's men stood completely apart from the rest, a handful of riders who looked as though they would piss their britches if the wrong word were spoken.

The ensuing silence was impenetrable.

And finally, the King of Scotia spoke. "Nay," he said at last. "I do not know this woman. She is not the one we seek."

Cat exhaled with relief.

There was another moment of silence, and then the MacKinnon asked, his tone low, but laced with sarcasm, "Are you certain?"

"Aye," David assured him once and for all, more firmly this time. "She is not the woman we seek. Come!" he directed his men, and they took their leave at once, though the MacKinnon's, the Brodies and Montgomerie and his men all remained.

Once it was certain that David would not return, Aidan came forward on his white horse, and bade her, "Next time you take a walk, my dear Cat, remind me to give you a leash," he said sardonically. "Now let us go home."

Cat's heart felt near to breaking.

She shook her head, refusing to move.

Gavin had had quite enough. He pushed his way through his brothers and through MacKinnon's men, moving into the forefront. "Nay!" he shouted. "You cannot take her!"

He strode directly before this man who called himself her brother but who spoke of putting her on a leash. He stood there in defiance, so angered that he had no notion that his breacan had come undone.

"I will hear it from her own two lips that she wishes to leave or you will have to cut me down to take her," he avowed.

To Gavin's utter surprise, the man began to laugh. His massive shoulders shook. His men all joined him.

He looked toward Cat to see that she was grinning too. She placed a hand to her mouth and wiggled her brows, urging him to look down.

When he did, he saw that his willy—still painted blue—was standing at attention, peeking out from beneath the folds of his breacan. He was hardly aroused, but with his temper flared, apparently his willy had something to say as well.

"That's a damned fine sword," Colin offered, clearing his throat and looking askance.

The MacKinnon choked on his laughter, and Piers did as well.

"Damn," Leith remarked. "Thank God none of our wives saw that monstrosity before our own!"

Gavin furrowed his brow, hardly amused. Nor was he embarrassed or the least deterred though he did cover his willy with his breacan.

He turned to Cat, only caring what she had to say this moment—his brothers bedamned. "I want to hear it from your own lips. Cat," he persisted. "If you tell me you must go, I willna stand in your way, but I hope you will stay... with me..."

Cat peered up at her brother, tears in her eyes.

After an interminable moment, Aidan nodded, and she turned to Gavin and nodded too, all her love shining in her eyes.

Gavin's heart felt near to bursting in that moment. Och, indeed, but if love was not some form of magik he didn't know what was. But his Cat was flesh and blood, and that pleased him more than he had words to say.

He fell to his knees and held out his hand for her to take, "Be my bride in truth," he entreated, and she came to him without hesitation, embracing him to her bosom.

"Apparently, another celebration is in order," The MacKinnon declared, his good humor restored.

"Aye, and I know where to find the *whiskie*," Colin quipped with a grin and a wink, and he waved Aidan and his men down from their horses, inviting them to follow him into the woods. Piers and his men went as well, but not before Piers ventured over to slap Gavin upon the back, complimenting him once more on his fine, sturdy roof.

Neither Gavin nor Cat heard a word any of them said.

Gavin kissed Cat soundly, whispering naughty promises in her ear—all the things he planned to do to her the instant they were alone once more.

And he realized suddenly that faith had set him out the door and that faith had brought him to this moment. He might not have understood exactly what he was seeking when he'd walked out that door, but somebody out there must have known...

At the edge of the woods, watching the band of men approach with whiskie on their minds and laughter in their hearts, at least six pairs of cat eyes blinked in unison... and in the gloaming—if you looked at them just so—it appeared they might be grinning.

Altogether they slunk away into the trees, leaving a dusting of dancing fireflies blinking in their wake.

Want to know more about Aidan and Cat?

Keep reading to learn more about HIGHLAND FIRE, book 1 of the Guardians of the Stones.

AFTERWORD

For years I have received letters from readers who cherished this series and the heroes and heroines whose stories are part of it. Highland Song is both an end to The Highland Brides and a beginning to a brand-new historical series. If you loved the characters from The Highland Brides, you can now follow them into a richer, more encompassing world that brings back favorite characters and introduces you to new ones.

Highland Fire is Aidan dún Scoti's story. If you're reading this note, you've already met Aidan in Highland Song. The year is 1125. The Picts are long gone, relegated to the annals of history, but one clan won't so easily forget the old ways. After the death of King Aed in 878, they fled into the mountains, taking with them the true Stone of Destiny, and there remained ... waiting for a worthy king to arise.

For two centuries, Aidan's people have harbored Scotland's most guarded secret deep in the Mounth, a rough range of hills on the southern edge of Strathdee in northeast Scotland. It's an unforgiving landscape, and his folk are steeped in the traditions of their past, painting themselves in the woad of their ancestors as a reminder of their noble beginnings.

They are the last of the "Painted Ones," the guardians of the Stone.

Now a struggle for power begins. The Highland tribes are fractured. David Ceann Mór, an English colluder, has claimed the throne of Scotia, but only a worthy king can possess the stone with the power to unite the Highland clans. Cursed by Aidan's people at birth for the sins of her father, Lìleas MacLaren is the one woman Aidan believes he is immune to ... offered in marriage as a guise for peace, she is also the one woman who can betray his clan's secret and bring them to war. Rich in history and lore, with a touch of magic, Highland Fire brings a legend to life.

If you haven't yet read The Highland Brides, you'll want to begin with Book 1, The MacKinnon's Bride, followed by Lyon's Gift, On Bended Knee and Lion Heart. If you've already read these beloved books, turn the page to download a FREE preview of Highland Fire.

HIGHLAND FIRE

Book 1 of The Guardians of the Stone

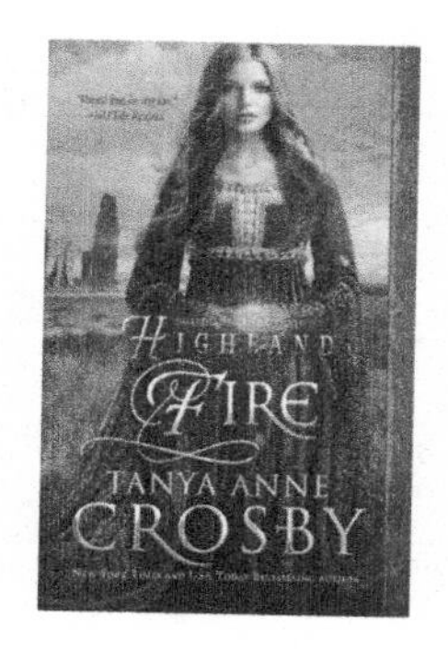

Did Aidan catch your eye? Read his story next. Highland Fire is now available FREE at all vendors. Keep reading to learn more about my new Guardians of the Stone series, beginning with HIGHLAND FIRE...

Cursed by Aidan's people at birth for the sins of her father, Lìleas MacLaren is the one woman Aidan believes he is immune to ... offered in marriage as a guise for peace, she is also the one woman who can betray his clan's secret and bring them to heel. Rich in history and lore, with a touch of magic, Highland Fire brings a legend to life in a brand new Highland series by *New York Times* Bestselling author Tanya Anne Crosby.

A HEARTFELT THANK YOU!

Thank you from the bottom of my heart for reading Highland Song! There are literally millions of titles out there, and I'm honored you decided to read one of mine.

I hope you'll follow Catrìona and her friends through the Guardians of the Brides series, and if you enjoyed this book, please consider posting a review. Reviews help other readers find books, and I sincerely appreciate all reviews, no matter how long or short.

Warmly,

Tanya Anne Crosby

CONNECTED SERIES

SERIES BIBLIOGRAPHY

Have you also read the Highland Brides and the Guardians of the Stone? While it's not necessary to read these past series to enjoy Daughters of Avalon, all three series are related with shared characters.

These books are Also available as Audiobooks

Start with The MacKinnon's Bride FREE

The Highland Brides

The MacKinnon's Bride

Lyon's Gift

On Bended Knee

Lion Heart

Highland Song

MacKinnon's Hope

The Guardians of the Stone

Once Upon a Highland Legend

Highland Fire

Highland Steel

Highland Storm

Maiden from the Mist

Also connected...

Angel of Fire

Once Upon a Kiss

Daughters of Avalon

The King's Favorite

A Winter's Rose

Fire Song

Rhiannon

GLOSSARY

Included here are just a few of the words and phrases I've used throughout my Scottish series. I often use learngaelic.net as a source, and just for fun, you might enjoy trying this Scottish translator: www.scotranslate.com.

Am Monadh Ruadh: the Cairngorms, literally the red hills distinguishing them from Am Monadh Liath, the grey hills

Aurochs: large wild cattle, now extinct

Bairn: baby

Bampot: idiot

Bean sìth: banshee:

Ben: mountain

Bliaut: men's and women's overgarment worn from the eleventh to the thirteenth century

Bhràthair: brother

bràthair-cèile: Brother-by-law

Breacan: short for breacan-an-feileadh, or great kilt

Bhrìghde: Sister of Cailleach Bheur

Bodachan Sabhaill: barn brownie

Brollachans: ghouls

Cailleach Bheur: the blue-faced mother of winter

Cairn: pile of stones, often built as a memorial or over a burial

Caoineag the Weeper: the banshee spirit who haunted the lochs and waterfalls. It was said she could be heard wailing before a death within a clan

Chreagach Mhor: great rocks

Clach-na-cinneamhain: stone of destiny

Claidheamh-mor: claymore

Clipe: a tell-tale

Corries: mountains, or hills

Crannóg: wooden dwellings the early Picts used as homes, often built over a body of water

Drogue: drug

Dwale: a drink made of nightshade or belladonna, often used for anesthesia

Fashious: troublesome

Gaol: jail

Geamhradh: Winter

Guarderobe/ garderobe: toilet

Keek stane: a scrying stone, or crystal ball

Ken: know

Leabhar: book

Loch: lake

Mac na h-Alba: son of Scotia

Minny: mother

Muckle: large

Pawky: having a sly sense of humor

Pechts: Picts

Quintain: a piece of training equipment used for jousting, often formed in the shape of a person

Reiver: raider on the English-Scottish border

Righ Art: the High King and Chief of Chiefs.

Sassenach: Englishman

Sùilean gorm: blue Eyes.

Scotia: Scotland, also known as Alba

Sìol Ailpín: the fractured Highland Clans who all claimed lineage to the first Ailpín king.

Tailard: an outsider, the enemy or an Englishman

Sluag: God of the Underworld

Siùrsach: whore

Targe: a circular shield used for defense

The Mounth: range of hills on the southern edge of Strathdee in northeast Scotland; bastardized version of Monadh. The mountain ranges are known as Monadh Liath and the Monadh Ruadh, which translated means Grey Mounth and the Red Mounth.

Trews: close-fitting tartan trousers

Uisge-beatha: whisky, literally means water of life

Vin aigre: vinegar or sour wine

Woad: a dye extracted from the woad plant

PHRASES

A bheil gàidhlig agaibh?: You speak the old tongue?

Ach ged a bha... tá grá agam duit: I have love for you.

An làmb a bheir, 's i a gheibh: The hand that gives is the hand that gets.

Buin mo chridhe dhuit: You are the love of my heart, or my heart belongs to you.

Cha d'dhùin doras nach d'fhosgail doras: No door ever closed, but another opened.

Cha deoch-slàint, i gun a tràghadh: It's no health if the glass is not emptied.

Cha togar m' fhearg gun dìoladh: No one can harm me unpunished.

Cnuic `is uillt `is Ailpeinich: Hills and streams

and MacAilpín.

Cuir claidheamh ann do truaill: Sheathe your sword.

Ceud mìle fàilte: A thousand welcomes.

Dia leat: Go with God.

Go raibh maith agat: may you have a thousand good things.

Faigh bàs: Go to hell.

Fàilte a mo dhachaidh: Welcome to my home.

Haud yer wheesht: Hush

Mac Bhàdhair fhuileach thu: Son of a cow's bloody afterbirth.

Mo cridhe: My heart

Mo dhuine: My man

Mo ghradh: My love

Mòran taing: Many thanks.

Oidhche math: Good night.

Tapadh leat: Thank you.

Tha e na Albannach gu a shàilean: He was a Scotsman to his bones.

Tha èigh sìth: I declare peace.

Tha gaol agam ort: I love you.

Tha i cho co-olcach: She is angry.

Tha, rud beag: A little.

Tha thu rùn-dìomhair, mo duine: You are a mystery, my husband.

'S mise le meas: yours respectfully

Slàinte mhòr agad: Great health to you all

Sùilean geala: bright eyes

ALSO BY TANYA ANNE CROSBY

A BRAND-NEW SERIES

DAUGHTERS OF AVALON

The King's Favorite

A Winter's Rose

Fire Song

Rhiannon

THE HIGHLAND BRIDES

The MacKinnon's Bride

Lyon's Gift

On Bended Knee

Lion Heart

Highland Song

MacKinnon's Hope

GUARDIANS OF THE STONE

Once Upon a Highland Legend

Highland Fire

Highland Steel

Highland Storm

Maiden of the Mist

THE MEDIEVALS HEROES

Once Upon a Kiss

Angel of Fire

Viking's Prize

The Impostor Series

The Impostor's Kiss

The Impostor Prince

Redeemable Rogues

Happily Ever After

Perfect In My Sight

McKenzie's Bride

Kissed by a Rogue

Mischief & Mistletoe

A Perfectly Scandalous Proposal

Anthologies & Novellas

Lady's Man

Married at Midnight

The Winter Stone

Romantic Suspense

Speak No Evil

Tell No Lies

Leave No Trace

Mainstream Fiction

The Girl Who Stayed

The Things We Leave Behind

Redemption Song

Everyday Lies

ABOUT THE AUTHOR

Tanya Anne Crosby is the New York Times and USA Today bestselling author of thirty novels. She has been featured in magazines, such as People, Romantic Times and Publisher's Weekly, and her books have been translated into eight languages. Her first novel was published in 1992 by Avon Books, where Tanya was hailed as "one of Avon's fastest rising stars." Her fourth book was chosen to launch the company's Avon Romantic Treasure imprint.

Known for stories charged with emotion and humor and filled with flawed characters Tanya is an award-winning author, journalist, and editor, and her novels have garnered reader praise and glowing critical reviews.

Tanya and her writer husband split their time between Charleston, SC, where she was raised, and northern Michigan, where the couple make their home.

For more information

www.tanyaannecrosby.com
tanya@tanyaannecrosby.com